"Who are you?" demanded Jack.

At a slow pace the figure walked toward him. Her high-heeled boots echoed on the cold, wet pavement. When she finally reached him, her face contorted into a pantomime of a smile. Her eyes were small and mean, and her nose upturned, as if she was sticking it against a window.

"My name is Miss Swine, I am the matron of Twilight Towers. And I've come to take your grandfather away," purred the lady.

ALSO BY
David Walliams

DEMON DENTIST

THE MIDNIGHT GANG

GRANDPA'S
GREAT ESCAPE

Written by

David Walliams

Illustrated by Tony Ross

HARPER
An Imprint of HarperCollinsPublishers

Grandpa's Great Escape

Text copyright © David Walliams 2015

Illustrations © Tony Ross 2015

All rights reserved. Printed in the United States of America.

No part of this book may be used or reproduced in any manner whatsoever with-out written permission except in the case of brief quotations embodied in critical articles and reviews. For information address HarperCollins Children's Books, a division of HarperCollins Publishers, 195 Broadway, New York, NY 10007.

www.harpercollinschildrens.com

Library of Congress Control Number: 2016952954

ISBN 978-0-06-256090-2

    19 20   BRR   10 9 8 7 6 5 4 3

❖

First U.S. paperback edition, 2018

This book is dedicated to
Sam & Phoebe, who are nearly always good.
With love, David x

HarperCollins *Children's Books*

presents

GRANDPA'S
GREAT ESCAPE

Written by.................................DAVID WALLIAMS

Illustrator...TONY ROSS

Editor...RUTH ALLTIMES

Desk Editor............................GEORGIA MONROE

Text Designer ....ELORINE GRANT

Cover Designer.................................KATE CLARKE

Sound....................TANYA BRENNAND-ROPER

Marketing..ALISON RUANE

AND NICOLA WAY

Promotion............................GERALDINE STROUD

AND SAM WHITE

Director....................................RACHEL DENWOOD

Mr. Walliams's Literary Agent.......PAUL STEVENS

AT INDEPENDENT

Executive Producer ....CHARLIE REDMAYNE

Produced by.................ANN-JANINE MURTAGH

*Special thanks to Charlotte Sluter and Laura Clouting at the
Imperial War Museum & Tim Granshaw, Matt Jones, Andy
Annabel, and Gerry Jones at Goodwood Aerodrome, & John
Nichol, RAF consultant.*

Up, up, and

away...

This is the tale of a boy called Jack
and his grandfather.

Once upon a time, Grandpa was a Royal Air Force pilot.

During World War II, he flew a Spitfire fighter plane.

Our story is set in 1983. This was a time before the internet and mobile telephones and computer games that could be played for weeks on end. In 1983, Grandpa was already an old man but his grandson, Jack, was just twelve years old.

This is Jack's mum and dad. Mum, Barbara, works at the cheese counter in the local supermarket. Dad, Barry, is an accountant.

Raj is the local newsagent.   Miss Verity is the history
teacher at Jack's school.

Detectives Beef and Bone
are a crime-fighting duo.

This is the town's vicar, Reverend Hogg.

This security guard works at the
Imperial War Museum in London.

Miss Swine is the matron of the local
old folk's home, *Twilight Towers*.

Some of the elderly residents there include
Mrs. Trifle, the Major, and the Rear Admiral.

These are some of the nurses who work at
Twilight Towers—Nurse Rose,
Nurse Daisy, and Nurse Blossom.

This is **Twilight Towers**.

Twilight Towers
Caring for your
unwanted old folk

This is a map of the town.

Church

Town Square

Railway Station

Raj's Flat

Grandpa's Flat

Twilight Towers

The Moors

School

Park

Raj's
Newsagent

Jack's
House

Prologue

One day, Grandpa began to forget things. It was little things at first. The old man would make himself a cup of tea and forget to drink it. Before long he would have lined up a dozen cups of cold tea on his kitchen table. Or he would run a bath and forget to turn off the taps, flooding his neighbor's flat downstairs. Or he would leave the house with the express purpose of buying a stamp, but return home with seventeen boxes of cornflakes. Grandpa didn't even like cornflakes.

Over time, Grandpa started to forget bigger things. What year it was. Whether his long-deceased wife, Peggy, was alive or not. One day, he even stopped recognizing his own son.

Most startling of all was that Grandpa completely forgot he was an old-age pensioner. The old man had always told his little grandson, Jack, stories of his adventures in the Royal Air Force all those years ago in World War II. Now these stories became more and more real to him. In fact, instead of just telling these stories, he began living them out. The present faded into scratchy black and white as the past burst into glorious color. It didn't matter where Grandpa was, or what he was doing, or whom he was with. In his mind, he was a dashing young pilot behind the controls of his Spitfire fighter plane.

All the people in Grandpa's life found this very difficult to understand.

Except one person.

His grandson, Jack.

Like all children, the boy loved to play, and it seemed to him that his grandpa was playing.

Jack realized all you had to do was play too.

1

Spam à la Custard

Jack was a child who was happiest alone in his bedroom. A naturally shy boy, he didn't have many friends. Instead of spending his days playing football in the park with all the other kids from school, he would stay inside assembling his prized collection of model airplanes. His favorites were from World War II—the Lancaster bomber, the Hurricane, and of course, his grandfather's old plane, the now legendary Spitfire. On the Nazi side, he had models of the Dornier bomber, the Junkers, and the Spitfire's deadly nemesis, the Messerschmitt.

With great care Jack would paint his model planes, then fix them to the ceiling with fishing wire. Suspended in the air, they looked like they were in the middle of a dramatic dogfight. At night, he would stare up at them from his bunk bed and drift off to sleep dreaming he was an RAF flying ace, just like his grandfather once was. The boy kept a picture of Grandpa by his bed. He was a young man in the old black-and-white photograph. It was taken sometime in 1940, at the height of the Battle of Britain. Grandpa was standing proudly in his RAF uniform.

In his dreams, Jack would go Up, *up, and away,* just like his grandfather had. The boy would have given everything he had, all of his past and all of his future, for one moment behind the controls of Grandpa's legendary Spitfire.

In his dreams, he would be a hero.
In his life, he felt like a zero.

The problem was that each day was exactly the same. He would go to school every morning, do his homework every afternoon, and eat his dinner in front of the television every night. If only he wasn't so shy. If only he had lots of friends. If only he could break free from his boring life.

The highlight of Jack's week was Sunday. That was the day his parents would leave him with his grandfather. Before the old man had become too confused, he would take his grandson on the most magical days out. The Imperial War Museum was the place they loved to visit the most. It was not too far away, in London, and was a treasure trove of all things military. Together the pair would marvel at the old warplanes hanging from the ceiling of the Great Room. The legendary Spitfire was, of course, their absolute favorite. Seeing her always brought Grandpa's memories of the war flooding back. He would share these stories with his grandson, who devoured every word. On the long bus

journey home, Jack would bombard the old man with hundreds and hundreds of questions...

"What's the fastest speed you ever went in your Spitfire?"

"Did you ever have to parachute out?"

"Which is the better fighter plane, the Spitfire or the Messerschmitt?"

Grandpa loved answering him. Often a crowd of children would gather around the old man on the top deck of the bus home to listen to these incredible tales.

"It was the summer of 1940," Grandpa would begin. "The height of the Battle of Britain. One night I was flying my Spitfire over the English Channel. I had become separated from my squadron. My fighter plane had taken a pounding in a dogfight. Now I was limping back to base. Then just behind me I heard machine guns. RAT TAT TAT! It was a Nazi Messerschmitt. Right on my tail! Again. RAT TAT TAT! It was just the two of us alone over the sea. That night would be an epic fight to the death…"

Grandpa enjoyed nothing more than sharing stories of his World War II adventures. Jack would listen intently; every little detail fascinated him. Over time, the boy became something of an expert on these old fighter planes. Grandpa would tell his grandson that he would make "an excellent pilot one day." This always made the boy burst with pride.

Then later in the day, if ever an old black-and-white war film was on the television, the pair would snuggle up on the sofa together in Grandpa's house and watch it. *Reach for the Sky* was one they watched over and over again. This classic told the story of a pilot who lost both his legs in a horrific accident before World War II. Despite this, Douglas Bader went on to become a legendary flying ace. Rainy Saturday afternoons were made for *Reach for the Sky*, or *One of Our Aircraft Is Missing*, or *The Way to the Stars* or *A Matter of Life and Death*. For Jack there was nothing better.

Sadly the food at Grandpa's home was always

diabolical. He called it "rations," as he had during the war. The old man only ever ate food from tins. For dinner he would select a couple at complete random from his larder and empty them into a pan together.

Corned beef with
pineapple chunks

Sardines and
rice pudding

Treacle sponge
with peas

Baked beans mixed
with tinned peaches

Diced carrots in condensed milk

Chocolate pudding
covered in
tomato soup

Pilchards with
spaghetti hoops

Steak-and-kidney
pudding and fruit
cocktail

Haggis topped with
cherries in syrup

And Grandpa's speciality, *Spam à la Custard*

The use of the French words gave it an air of poshness it did not deserve. Fortunately the boy didn't come for the food.

World War II was the most important time in Grandpa's life. It was a time when brave Royal Air Force pilots like him fought for their country in the Battle of Britain. The Nazis were planning an invasion, a plot they called Operation Sea Lion. However, without being able to secure power over the skies to protect their troops on the ground, the Nazis were never able to put their plan into action. Day after day, night after night, RAF pilots like Grandpa risked their lives to keep the people of Britain free from being captured by the Nazis.

So instead of reading a book to his grandson at bedtime, the old man would tell the boy of his real-life adventures during the war. His stories were more thrilling than any you could find in a book.

"One more tale, Grandpa! Please!" the boy begged on one such night. "I want to hear about when you were shot down by the Luftwaffe and had to crash-land into the English Channel!"

"It's late, young Jack," Grandpa replied. "You go to sleep. I promise I will tell you that tale and plenty more in the morning."

"But—"

"I'll meet you in your dreams, Squadron Leader," said the old man as he kissed Jack tenderly on the forehead. "Squadron Leader" was his nickname for his grandson. "I'll see you in the skies. Up, *up*, *and away.*"

"Up, *up*, *and away!*" the boy repeated before drifting off to sleep in Grandpa's spare room, dreaming he too was a fighter pilot. Time spent with Grandpa couldn't have been more perfect.

But that was all about to change.

2

Slippers

Over time, Grandpa's mind began transporting him back to his days of glory more and more. By the time our story begins, the old man completely believed that it was still World War II. Even though the war had ended decades before.

Grandpa had become very confused, a condition that affects some elderly people. It was serious, and sadly there was no known cure. Instead, it seemed likely it would continue to worsen, until one day Grandpa might not even be able to remember his own name.

But as ever in life, wherever there is tragedy, you can often find comedy. In recent times the old man's condition had led to some very funny moments. On Bonfire Night, Grandpa insisted everyone go down to the air-raid shelter at once when the next-door neighbors started letting off fireworks in the garden. Or there was the time when Grandpa cut a wafer-thin chocolate mint into four pieces with his penknife and shared it out with the family because of "rationing."

Most memorable of all was the time Grandpa decided that a shopping trolley at the supermarket was really a Lancaster bomber. He hurtled down the aisles on a top secret mission, hurling huge bags of flour. These "bombs" exploded everywhere— over the food, over the tills, even covering the haughty supermarket manageress from head to toe.

She looked like a powdery ghost. The cleanup operation lasted many weeks. Grandpa was banned from the supermarket for life.

Sometimes Grandpa's confusion could be more upsetting. Jack had never met his grandmother. This was because she had died nearly forty years ago. It had been one night toward the end of the war in a Nazi bombing raid over London. At the time, Jack's father was a newborn baby. However, when Jack stayed at his grandfather's tiny flat, the old man would sometimes call for his "Darling Peggy" as if she was in the next room. Tears would well in the boy's eyes. It was heartbreaking.

Despite everything, Grandpa was an incredibly proud man. For him everything had to be "just so."

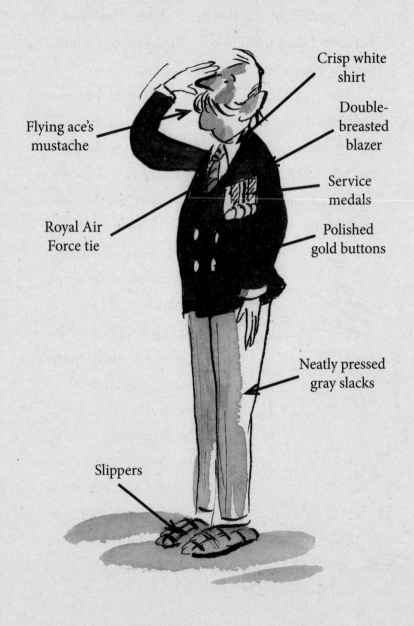

Flying ace's
mustache

Royal Air
Force tie

Crisp white
shirt

Double-
breasted
blazer

Service
medals

Polished
gold buttons

Neatly pressed
gray slacks

Slippers

He was always impeccably dressed in a uniform of double-breasted blazer, crisp white shirt, and neatly pressed gray slacks. A maroon, silver, and blue–striped Royal Air Force tie was forever knotted neatly around his neck. As was the fashion with many World War II pilots, he favored a dashing flying ace's mustache. It was a thing of wonder. The mustache was so long it connected to his sideburns. It was like a beard but with the chin bit missing. Grandpa would twizzle the ends of his mustache for hours, until they stuck out at just the right angle.

The one thing that would give Grandpa's confused state of mind away was his choice of footwear. Slippers. The old man no longer wore shoes. Now he always forgot to put them on. Whatever the weather, in rain, sleet, and snow, he would be sporting his brown-checked slippers.

Of course Grandpa's eccentric behavior made the grown-ups worry. Sometimes Jack would pretend to go to bed but instead creep out of his bedroom and sit at the top of the stairs in his pajamas. There he would listen to his mother and father downstairs in the kitchen, discussing Grandpa. They would use big words that Jack didn't understand to describe the old man's "condition." Then Mum and Dad would argue about Grandpa being put in an old folk's home. The boy hated hearing his grandfather talked about in this way, as if he was some sort of problem. However, being only twelve years old, Jack felt powerless to do anything.

But none of this stopped Jack from adoring hearing stories about the old man's wartime adventures, even though these tales had become so real to Grandpa now that the pair would act them out. They were *Boy's Own* adventures, stories of derring-do.

Grandpa had an ancient wooden record player the size of a bath. On it he would play booming orchestral music, with the volume as high as it would go. Military bands were his favorite, and together Jack and his grandfather would listen to huge classical pieces like "Rule, Britannia!," "Land of Hope and Glory" or the "Pomp and Circumstance" marches way into the night. Two old armchairs would become their cockpits. As the music soared, so did they in their

imaginary fighter planes. A Spitfire for Grandpa and a Hurricane for Jack. *Up, up, and away,* they would go. Together they would fly high above the clouds, outwitting enemy aircraft. Every Sunday night the pair of flying aces would win the Battle of Britain, without even leaving the old man's tiny flat.

Together Grandpa and Jack inhabited their own world and had countless imaginary adventures.

However, the night our story starts, a real-life adventure was about to begin.

3

A Waft of Cheese

This particular evening, Jack was asleep in his bedroom, dreaming he was a World War II pilot, as he did every night. He was sitting behind the controls of his Hurricane, taking on a squadron of deadly Messerschmitts, when he heard the distinct sound of a telephone ringing.

RING RING RING RING.

That was strange, he thought, there weren't any telephones on board 1940s fighter planes. Yet still the telephone kept ringing.

RING RING RING RING.

The boy woke up with a start. As he sat up in bed he banged his head on his model Lancaster bomber that was suspended from the ceiling.

"Ow!" he cried. He checked the time on the nickel-plated RAF pilot's watch his grandfather had given him.

2:30 a.m.

Who on earth was calling the house at this hour?

The boy leaped down from his top bunk and opened his bedroom door. Downstairs in the hall, he could hear his mother talking on the telephone.

"No, he hasn't turned up here," she said.

After a few moments, Mum spoke again. Her familiar tone convinced Jack that she must be talking to his father. "So no sign of the old man at all? Well what are you going to do, Barry? I know he's your father! But you can't stay out all night looking for him!"

Jack couldn't remain silent for a moment longer. From the top of the stairs he cried, "What's happened to Grandpa?"

Mum looked up. "Oh, well done, Barry, now Jack's woken up!" She put her hand over the receiver. "Go back to bed this instant, young man! You've got school in the morning!"

"I don't care!" replied the boy with defiance. "What's happened to Grandpa?"

Mum returned to the telephone call. "Barry, call me back in two minutes. It's all going off here now and all!" With that she slammed down the receiver.

"What's happened?" demanded the boy again as he ran down the stairs to join his mother.

Mum sighed theatrically as if all the woes of the world were on her shoulders. She did that a lot. It was at this exact moment that Jack realized he could smell cheese. Not just normal cheese. **Smelly cheese,** **blue cheese,** runny cheese, MOLDY CHEESE, cheesy cheese. His mother worked at the cheese counter of the local supermarket, and wherever she went, a strong waft of cheese came with her.

Both stood in the hall in their nightclothes, Jack in his stripy blue pajamas, and his mother in her pink fluffy nightgown. Her hair was in curlers and she had thick smears of face cream on her cheeks, forehead, and nose. She often left it on overnight. Jack wasn't sure exactly why. Mum thought of herself as quite a beauty, and often claimed to be the "glamorous face of cheese," if such a thing was possible.

Mum flicked on the light and they both blinked for a moment at the sudden brightness.

"Your grandpa's gone missing again!"

"Oh no!"

"Oh yes!" The woman sighed once more. It was clear she was worn out by the old man. Sometimes she would even roll her eyes at Grandpa's war stories, as if she was bored. This bothered Jack greatly. Grandpa's stories were infinitely more exciting than being told about the week's bestselling cheese. "Me and your father were woken up by a phone call around midnight."

"From who?"

"His neighbor downstairs, you know, that newsagent man…"

After his big house had become too much for him, Grandpa had moved last year to a little flat above a shop. Not just any shop. A newsagent's shop. Not just any newsagent's shop. Raj's.

"Raj?" replied Jack now.

"Yeah, that's his name. Raj said he thought he heard your grandpa's door bang around midnight. He knocked on his door, but there was no answer. The poor man got himself in a terrible panic, so he called here."

"Where's Dad?"

"He jumped in the car and has been out searching for your grandpa for the past couple of hours."

"Couple of hours?!" The boy couldn't believe what he was hearing. "Why on earth didn't you wake me?"

Mum sighed AGAIN. Tonight was turning into something of a sigh-a-thon. "Me and your dad know how fond you are of him, so we didn't want you to worry, did we?"

"Well, I am worried!" replied the boy. In truth  he felt a lot closer to his exciting grandfather than he did to anyone  else in the family, including his mother and father. Time spent with Grandpa was always precious.

"We're all worried!" replied Mum.

"I am really worried."

"Well, we're all really worried."

"Well, I am really really worried."

"Well, we're all really really really worried. Now please let's not have a competition about who is the **most worried!**" she shouted angrily.

Jack could tell his mother was becoming increasingly stressed, so he thought it best not to reply to that last remark, even though he was really really really worried.

"I've told your dad a hundred times your grandpa needs to be in an old folk's home!"

"Never!" said the boy. He knew the old man better than anyone. "Grandpa would absolutely hate that!"

Grandpa—or Wing Commander Bunting as he was known during the war—was far too proud to spend the last of his days with a lot of old dears doing crosswords and knitting.

Mum shook her head and sighed. "Jack, you are too young to understand."

Like all children, Jack hated being told this. But now wasn't the time to argue. "Mum, please. Let's go and look for him."

"Are you NUTS? It's freezing tonight!" replied the woman.

"But we have to do something! Grandpa is out there somewhere, lost!"

RING RING RING RING.

Jack lunged for the telephone, lifting the receiver before his mother could. "Dad? Where are you? The town square? Mum just said we should come out and help you look for Grandpa," he lied, as his mother gave him an angry look. "We'll be there as soon as we can."

The boy put the receiver down, and took his mum by the hand.

"Grandpa needs us..." he said.

Jack opened the door and the pair ran out into the darkness.

4

Secondhand Trike

The town was eerily unfamiliar at night. All was dark and quiet. It was the deepest winter. A mist hung in the air, and the ground was moist after a heavy downpour of rain.

Dad had taken the car, so Jack pedaled along the road on his trike. This trike was only meant for toddlers. In fact, the boy had been given the trike secondhand for his third birthday and had outgrown it many years ago. However, his family didn't have enough money to buy him a new bike, so he had to make do.

Mum stood on the back, holding on to his shoulders. If any of his classmates from school had seen him giving his mother a lift on his trike, Jack knew he would have to go and live alone in a dark and distant cave for all eternity.

Grandpa's military band music played out in Jack's head as he pedaled as fast as he could down the street. For a toddler's trike, it was a deceptively heavy beast, especially with his mother standing on the back, her fluffy pink nightgown blowing in the wind.

As the wheels turned around on his trike so did the thoughts in Jack's mind. The boy was closer to the old man than anybody; surely he could guess where his grandfather was?

Without seeing another soul on the way, the pair finally arrived at the town square. A pathetic sight greeted them.

Dad was in his pajamas and dressing gown, hunched over the steering wheel of the family's little brown car. Even from a distance, Jack could see the poor man couldn't take much more of this. Grandpa had gone missing from his flat seven times in the past couple of months.

When he heard the trike approach, Dad sat up in his seat. Jack's father was wiry and pale. He wore glasses and looked older than he was. His son often wondered whether being married to Mum had added years to the poor chap.

With the sleeve of his dressing gown, Dad wiped his eyes. It was clear he had been crying. Jack's father was an accountant. He spent all day doing long boring sums and didn't find it easy to express his feelings. Instead, he would bottle things up. However, Jack knew his dad loved his father very much, even though he was nothing like him. It was as if the love of adventure had skipped a generation. The old man's head was in the clouds, while his son's head was buried in books of figures.

"Are you all right, Dad?" asked the boy, breathless from pedaling.

As his father wound down the window to talk to them, the handle came off in his hand. The car was ancient and rusty, and bits often fell off.

"Yes, yes, I'm fine," Dad lied, as he held the handle aloft, not quite sure what to do with it.

"So no sign of the old man?" asked Mum, already knowing the answer.

"No," replied Dad softly. He turned away from them and stared straight ahead to hide how upset he was. "I've looked all over town for him for the past few hours."

"Did you look in the park?" asked Jack.

"Yes," replied Dad.

"The railway station?"

"Yes. It was all locked up for the night, but there was no one outside."

Suddenly Jack had an inspired thought, and couldn't get the words out fast enough. "The War Memorial?!"

The man returned his gaze to his son, and shook

his head sorrowfully. "That's the first place I looked."

"Well, that's it then!" announced Mum. "Let's call the police. They can stay out all night looking for him. I am going back to bed! We have a big promotion on our Wensleydale at the cheese counter tomorrow and I need to look my best!"

"No!" said Jack. From secretly listening to his parents' conversations about Grandpa at night, the boy knew this could spell disaster. Once the police were involved, questions would be asked. Forms would have to be filled in. The old man would become "a problem." Doctors would poke and prod him, and because of his condition no doubt Grandpa would be sent straight to an old folk's home. To someone like his grandfather, who had lived a life of freedom and adventure, it would be like a prison sentence. They simply had to find him.

"Up, *up*, and away..." muttered the boy.

"What, son?" replied Dad, mystified.

"That's what Grandpa always says to me when we are playing pilots together in his flat. As we take off he always says, 'Up, *up*, and away.'"

"So...?" demanded Mum. She rolled her eyes and sighed at the same time. Double whammy.

"So..." replied Jack. "I bet that's where Grandpa is. Up high somewhere."

The boy thought long and hard about which was the tallest building in town. After a moment it dawned on him. **"Follow me!"** Jack exclaimed, before speeding off down the road, pedaling his trike furiously.

5

Loon in the Moon

The highest point in the town was in fact the church spire. It was something of a local landmark and could be seen for miles around. Jack had a hunch that Grandpa might have tried to climb up there. When he had gone missing before, he had often been found somewhere high up, atop a climbing frame, up a ladder, even once on the roof of a double-decker bus. It was as if he needed to touch the sky as he had done all those years ago as an RAF pilot.

As the church came into view, there was the distinct silhouette of a man sitting on top of the spire. He was perfectly framed by the glow of a low silvery moon.

From the moment Jack saw his grandfather he knew exactly what the old man thought he was doing. Flying his Spitfire.

At the foot of the tall church was the short vicar.

Reverend Hogg had a rather obvious comb-over. What hair he had left was dyed so black it was blue. His eyes were as small as penny coins, hidden behind black-framed glasses. The vicar's glasses rested on his upturned piggy nose, which he was forever sticking in the air so he could look down it at people.

Jack's family did not go to church regularly, so the boy had only seen the vicar out and about in the local town. But once he had seen Reverend Hogg carrying a crate of expensive-looking champagne from the off-license. On another occasion, Jack could have sworn he saw the man cruising past in a brand-new Lotus Esprit sports car, puffing on a big fat cigar. *Weren't vicars meant to help the poor*, Jack couldn't help wondering, *not lavish money on themselves*?

This being the middle of the night, Reverend Hogg was still wearing his bedclothes. The vicar's pajamas and dressing gown were made of the finest silk, and he was sporting a pair of red velvet slippers which were monogrammed "C of E" (for Church of England). Around his wrist was curled a chunky diamond-encrusted gold watch. He was clearly a man who had a taste for the high life.

"GET DOWN FROM THERE!" barked Reverend Hogg at the old man, just as the family ran through the graveyard.

"IT'S MY GRANDPA!" shouted Jack, once again breathless from having pedaled so hard on his trike. Reverend Hogg reeked of cigars, a smell the boy could not stomach, and instantly he felt a little queasy.

"Well, what on earth is he doing on MY church roof?!"

"I am sorry, vicar!" yelled Dad. "It's my father. He gets confused…"

"Then he should be under lock and key! He has already dislodged some of the lead off MY roof!"

From behind the gravestones, a gang of tough-looking men appeared. They all had shaved heads, tattoos, and teeth missing. From their overalls and spades, Jack assumed they must be gravediggers. Though it seemed strange that they were digging graves in the dead of night.

One of the gravediggers handed the vicar a torch,

which he shone straight into the old man's eyes. **"COME DOWN THIS INSTANT!"**

Yet still Grandpa did not respond. As usual he was in a world of his own.

"Rudder steady. Holding on course, over?" he said instead. It was clear he did indeed believe he was high up in the skies piloting his beloved Spitfire.

"Wing Commander to base, over?" he went on.

"What on earth is he on about?" demanded Reverend Hogg, before muttering under his breath, "The man is a complete loon."

One of the gravediggers, a big, burly man with a tattoo of a spider's web on his neck spoke up. "Shall I fetch your air rifle, Reverend? A few shots should scare him down in no time!"

His fellow gravediggers snickered at the thought.

Air rifle! The boy needed to think fast if his grandfather was going to make it down to earth safely. "No! Let me try!" Jack had an idea. "This is base, over," he called up.

All the grown-ups looked at him in disbelief.

"Wing Commander

Bunting reading you loud and clear," replied Grandpa. "Current cruising altitude is 2,000 feet, ground speed of 320 miles per hour. Have been circling all night but no sign of enemy aircraft, over."

"Then your mission is accomplished, sir, return to base, over," said Jack.

"Roger that!"

From the foot of the church the group below looked up in incredulity as the old man—still sat on the church spire—made an imaginary landing. Grandpa was completely convinced he was behind the controls of his fighter plane; he even mimed turning the engine off. Next he slid open the invisible canopy, and climbed out.

Dad closed his eyes. He was so scared his father was going to fall, he couldn't watch a moment longer. Jack's eyes were wide-open in terror. He didn't dare blink.

The old man clambered down the spire, on to the roof. For a moment he stood still on the narrow peak, then without a care in the world he walked along it. But the piece of lead he had dislodged on his way up had left a dent in the roof, so after just a few paces...

TRIP!

...Grandpa went flying through the air.

"Nooo!" cried Jack.
"DAD!" shouted Dad.

"ARGH!" screamed Mum. The vicar and gravediggers looked on with grim fascination.

The old man slid down the roof, dislodging some more of the vicar's precious lead tiles along the way.

SMASH! SMASH!

As they crashed on the ground, Grandpa hurtled over the roof edge.

WHOOSH!

But at that moment, without making a fuss, the old man managed to grab on to the guttering and came to a stop. His thin legs swayed in the night air,

his slippers bumping against the stained glass window of the church.

"Careful of MY window!" shouted the vicar.

"Hold on, Dad!" called out Jack's father.

"I told you we should have called the police," added Mum unhelpfully.

"I have a christening at the church first thing tomorrow!" exclaimed Reverend Hogg. "We can't be scrubbing bits of your grandfather off the ground all morning!"

"Dad? DAD?" called out Jack's father.

Jack thought for a moment. If he didn't act fast, his poor grandpa was sure to plummet to his death.

"He won't respond to being called that," said the boy. "Let me." Jack then projected his voice once more. "Wing Commander? This is Squadron Leader!"

"Ah, there you are, old boy!" Grandpa called down from the guttering. Jack's pretend name had now become real to the old man. Grandpa believed the boy was a fellow airman.

"Just make your way along the aircraft's wing to your right," called up Jack.

Grandpa paused for a moment, before answering, "Roger that." A moment later he started shimmying

his hands along the guttering.

Jack's approach was utterly

unexpected. Yet it worked. You had to enter Grandpa's world if you wanted to get through to him.

Jack spotted a drainpipe running down the side of the church. "Now, Wing Commander, you see that pole to your right?" shouted the boy.

"Yes, Squadron Leader."

"Hold on tight and slowly slide down it, sir."

Both Mum and Dad gasped and covered their mouths as Grandpa swung like an acrobat from the guttering to the pipe. For a moment all was still as he held on tight at the top. However, his weight must have been too much for the pipe. Suddenly it came loose from the wall and started rapidly bending downwards.

CREAK went the pipe.

Had Jack said the wrong thing? Was he now sending his beloved grandfather hurtling toward the ground?

"NOOOOOOO!" cried the boy.

6

A Runaway Bulldozer

To Jack's relief, instead of snapping, the church drainpipe bent down slowly under the old man's weight.

TWONG!

Eventually it placed him safely on the ground.

As soon as his slippers touched the wet grass of the graveyard, Grandpa marched over to the assembled group and gave them a salute. "Fall out, men."

Mum looked more than a little offended.

"Wing Commander?" said the boy. "Please let me escort you to your car. We'll drive you back to your quarters shortly."

"Jolly good show, old boy," replied Grandpa.

Jack took him by the arm and led him to the family's rusty old car. As he opened the door, the handle came clean off. He put his grandfather safely in the backseat and closed the door once more so the old man could get warm on this chilly winter night.

As he ran back across the graveyard, Jack heard Reverend Hogg saying to his parents, "That man isn't all there! He needs to be locked up…"

"He is fine, thank you very much!" said Jack, jumping in on the conversation.

The vicar looked down at the boy and smiled, baring his teeth like a shark before it takes a bite. Jack watched as a thought seemed to cross the man's mind. Suddenly the vicar's tone of voice completely changed. "Mr. and Mrs....?" he began again, now sounding kind and caring.

"Bunting," replied Mum and Dad at the same time.

"Mr. and Mrs. Bunting, in my many years as vicar, I have brought a great deal of comfort to the old folk of this parish, and I would love to help your elderly relative."

"Oh, would you?" said Mum, immediately charmed by this slippery fish.

"Yes, Mrs. Bunting. In fact, I know an absolutely smashing place he could be sent to. It recently opened after the previous old folk's home was ACCIDENTALLY demolished by a runaway bulldozer."

Out of the corner of his eye, Jack caught the gravediggers smirking at this. The boy couldn't put his finger on it exactly, but he felt like something was very wrong here.

"Yes, we read about that in the local paper," replied Dad. "A runaway bulldozer? Who would have thought it?"

"The good Lord moves in mysterious ways," replied Reverend Hogg.

"You know what, Mr. Vicar?" continued Mum. "I have been saying it to these two until I've gone blue in the face. And Jill at the cheese counter agrees."

"So you work at a cheese counter?" inquired Reverend Hogg. "I thought I could smell Stilton."

"Yes!" replied Mum. "One of our speciality cheeses. It's such a beautiful aroma, isn't it, Mr. Vicar? Like perfume really."

Dad rolled his eyes.

"Anyway, so Jill is of the same mind," continued Mum again. "An old folk's home would be the best place for him."

Jack looked at his father and shook his head vigorously, but the man pretended not to notice his son.

"Is it a nice place?" asked Dad.

"Mr. Bunting, I wouldn't be recommending it if it wasn't," purred the vicar. "It's better than nice. It's like Disneyland for old people. The only problem is, it's so popular…"

"Is it?" asked Dad, now also completely sucked in by the man's patter.

"Yes, it's very hard to get a place," said Reverend Hogg.

"Well, that's settled then," said Jack. "He can't go anyway."

The vicar continued without pausing for breath. "Fortunately I know the matron who runs the place rather well. Lovely woman, Miss Swine, and rather attractive, I am sure you will agree when you meet her. If you wanted I could ask her if your dear old grandpa could jump the queue."

"That's very kind of you, Mr. Vicar," said Mum.

"What's this place called?" asked Dad.

"Twilight Towers," replied Reverend Hogg. "It's not far from here. Just on the edge of the moors. I could call Miss Swine now and ask one of my boys here to run him up there tonight, if you like…?" The vicar indicated his burly gang of gravediggers.

"That would save us the bother," agreed Mum.

"NO!" protested Jack.

Dad tried to steer the family toward a middle

ground. "Well, thank you so much, Vicar, we'll have a think about it."

"No, we won't!" protested Jack. "My grandpa's never going into a home! NEVER!"

With that, Dad started ushering his wife and son toward the car, where Grandpa had been waiting patiently.

But as Jack was trailing behind, and just out of earshot of his parents, the vicar turned to him and hissed, "We'll see about that, young man…"

7

Disneyland for Old People

It was nearly dawn by the time they were all home. Jack managed to convince his parents that it was for the best that Grandpa stayed with the family for the rest of the night, rather than return alone to his flat.

The boy put it in terms he thought his grandfather would understand. "Because of enemy reconnaissance missions in the area, the Air Chief Marshal has ordered you to move quarters."

Before long, Grandpa was fast asleep on the bottom bunk in the boy's bedroom, snoring for England. ZZZzzz! ZZZZZZ! Zzz! ZZZzz! The ends of the old man's mustache blew up and down with each breath.

Unable to sleep, and with his heart still pounding in his chest from the night's adventure, the boy slid down silently from the top bunk. As was often the case, he could hear muffled voices from downstairs and wanted to listen to what his parents were saying. Expertly he opened his bedroom door without making a sound. He sat on the carpet at the top of the stairs, one of his ears pushed between two bannisters.

"Mr. Vicar was right," said Mum. "A home is the best place for him."

"I'm really not sure, Barbara," protested Dad. "Grandpa wouldn't like it."

"Did you not listen to the nice man? What did Mr. Vicar say about Twilight Towers?"

"He said it was like 'Disneyland for old people'?"

"Exactly! Now I don't imagine there are roller coasters or log flumes or someone dressed up as a giant mouse, but it sounds wonderful."

"But—"

"The vicar is a man of the church! He would never lie!" snapped Mum.

"Maybe it is like he said. But Grandpa's always

been such a free spirit."

"Yes!" Mum replied with a note of triumph in her voice. "Such a free spirit that we find him up on the church roof in the middle of the night!"

There was silence for a moment. Dad did not have an answer for this.

"Listen, Barry, what else can we do?" continued Mum. "The old man's becoming a danger to himself. He very nearly fell off that roof and died!"

"I know, I know…" Dad muttered.

"Well?"

"Maybe it is for the best."

"That's settled once and for all then. We can drop him off at Twilight Towers tomorrow."

As Jack listened at the top of the stairs, a tear welled in his eye, and rolled very slowly down his cheek.

8

Spit It Out!

True to form at breakfast the next morning, Grandpa was acting as if nothing out of the ordinary had happened. As he sat happily tucking into his fried eggs and bacon in the kitchen of the family home, it was clear that the old man had no memory whatsoever of the past night's dramatic events.

"More bread! Quickly, please, Charlady, chop chop!" he ordered.

Mum did not appreciate being treated like some kind of servant. "Charlady" was what posh people called their cleaners in the olden days. She looked to her husband to do something, but Dad pretended to read the paper.

Two slices of white bread were slammed down on the table and within a moment Grandpa began mopping up all the grease on his plate.

As he devoured the bread, he announced, "I'll have the bread fried next time, please, Charlady!"

"Oh, will you now?!" replied Mum sarcastically.

Jack couldn't help but smile, though he tried to hide it.

The old man slurped his tea, followed by a, "Down the hatch!" Grandpa said that whenever he drank anything.

"Mum, Dad, I've been thinking," announced the boy. "As I was up so late, I think it's best I don't go to school today."

"What?" replied Mum.

"Yes. I can stay here and look after Grandpa. In fact, I should probably take the whole week off!"

Jack didn't like school much. He had just turned twelve, so he had been sent off to big school. He hadn't made any friends there yet. All the other kids seemed to be only interested in the latest pop star or silly gadget. This being 1983, many of the kids spent their lessons fiddling with their Rubik's Cubes under their desks. Jack couldn't find a single person who had a passion for model airplanes. On his first day, he was laughed at by some older boys for even mentioning them. So Jack learned to keep his mouth shut.

"You are going to school today, young man!" Mum always called her son "young man" when he had done something wrong. "You tell him, Barry!"

Dad looked up from his newspaper. "Well, it was very late last night…"

"BARRY!"

The man suddenly thought better of disagreeing with his wife and his sentence quickly changed tack. "…But of course you shouldn't miss school. And in the future, please do absolutely everything your mother says." Finally he added a rather mournful, "I know I do."

Next, the woman gave her husband a rather unsubtle poke on the shoulder. It was clear she wanted him to make the big announcement about Grandpa. As Dad did not immediately respond, she poked him again. This time it was so hard he actually went, "Ow!"

"Bar-ry…" she prompted. Mum always said Dad's name in that strange elongated way when she was trying to get him to do something.

Dad put down his paper and folded it slowly to put off speaking as long as he could. He looked straight at his father.

Jack feared the worst.

Was this the moment when Dad would tell Grandpa that he was going to be sent to *Twilight Towers*?

"Now, Dad. You know we all love you very much and only want the best for you…"

Grandpa slurped his mug of tea noisily. It wasn't clear whether he had heard what his son had said at all, as there was no flicker in his eyes. Dad started again, speaking slower and louder than before. "Are… you… lis-ten-ing… to… me?"

"Spit it out, Cadet!" replied Grandpa. Jack smirked. The boy loved that his grandfather gave Dad a much lower rank than him. In fact, the lowest rank there was.

RAF officer ranks were as follows:

Officer Cadet (the lowest of the low)

Acting Pilot Officer (not quite the lowest of the low)

Pilot Officer (now you are getting somewhere)

Flying Officer (could still do better)

Flight Lieutenant (not bad)

Squadron Leader (even better)

Wing Commander (even better than that)

Group Captain (ooh, you have done well)

Air Commodore (look at you!)

Air Vice Marshal (your mum must be very proud)

Air Marshal (oooh!)

Air Chief Marshal (nearly there, dear)

Marshal of the Royal Air Force (Mr. Big Pants)

Dad (or "Officer Cadet Bunting" as Grandpa called him) took a deep breath and started again. "Well, we all love you very much, and were thinking, well, it was the... er... Charlady..."

Mum glared at Dad.

"...I mean Barbara's idea really. But after last night we both agree. We thought it might be best if you went into..."

Jack had to say something, anything. He needed to buy his grandpa some time. So before Dad could finish his sentence he blurted: "...School with me today!"

9

Colored Chalks

Jack had been petitioning his history teacher, Miss Verity, to be allowed to bring Grandpa into her class all term. At his new school, they had started studying World War II. Who better to learn about it from than someone who had actually been there? What's more, all the other kids could see how cool his grandfather was. Maybe then having a collection of model airplanes wouldn't be so sad after all?

Miss Verity was a tall, thin woman who wore long skirts down to her ankles and frilly blouses up to her chin. Her spectacles hung from her neck on a silver chain. She was one of those teachers who somehow managed to make an exciting subject deathly dull. History should be thrilling, with its stories of heroes and villains who shaped the destiny of the world. Bloodthirsty kings and queens. Daring battles.

Unspeakable methods of torture.

Sadly, Miss Verity's method of teaching was mind-numbing. All the lady would do was write dates and names in her beloved colored chalks up on the blackboard. Then her pupils would have to copy everything down into their exercise books. **"Facts! Facts! Facts!"** she would recite as she scribbled away. Facts were all she cared about. One particular history lesson, all the boys from her class clambered out of the window for a crafty game of footy on the playground. Miss Verity didn't even notice they were gone, as she never turned around from her blackboard.

Convincing the history teacher to allow Grandpa into the classroom at some point had not been an easy task. In the end, Jack had to bribe her with a set of colored chalks from the local newsagent's shop. Fortunately for the boy, the shop owner, Raj, had sold the set of "luxury" chalks as part of one of his special offers. They had come free with an out-of-date box of fudge.

It was lucky that history was the second lesson of the day, as Grandpa made his grandson rather late for

school. First, it took a while to convince
the old man that when Jack had said
"school," he did of course mean an RAF
"flying school," and not just the local
comprehensive. Second, the "shortcut"
through the park turned out to be
something of a "long cut." Grandpa had
insisted on climbing to the very top of the
tallest tree in the park so he could "keep
an eye out for enemy aircraft." Coming
down took a great deal longer than going
up, and in the end Jack had to borrow a
ladder from a nearby window cleaner to
coax his grandfather to the ground.

When the pair eventually passed
through the school gates, Jack looked at

his RAF-issue watch and realized his history lesson had started ten minutes ago! If there was one thing Miss Verity could not abide, it was lateness. All eyes turned to the boy as he entered the classroom. Jack went bright red with embarrassment. He hated being the center of attention.

"Why are you late, boy?" barked Miss Verity, spinning around from her blackboard.

Before Jack could reply, Grandpa stepped into the classroom.

"Wing Commander Bunting at your service, madam," he said with a salute, before bowing his head and kissing the teacher's hand.

"Miss Verity," she replied, giggling and covering her mouth nervously. The teacher was obviously flattered by Grandpa's gallantry. It might have been some time since a gentleman had made a fuss of her in this way. That the teacher giggled made the class giggle too. To silence them, Miss Verity gave the children one of her famous death stares. These were so chilling that they always worked in an instant.

"Please take a seat, Mr. Bunting. I had absolutely no idea you were coming today!" She glared at Jack. The boy offered his teacher a warm smile. "But you are here, so let's make the best of it. I believe you are going to tell us all about your life as a World War II fighter pilot?"

"Roger!" replied Grandpa.

The teacher checked behind her, in case someone called Roger had entered the room. "Who's Roger?"

"It means yes, miss," called out Jack.

"Pop your hand in the air if you have something to say, boy," she snapped, before turning back to Jack's grandpa. "We have just begun studying the Battle of Britain. Please, can you tell us something of your personal experience of this?"

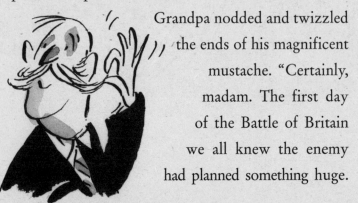

Grandpa nodded and twizzled the ends of his magnificent mustache. "Certainly, madam. The first day of the Battle of Britain we all knew the enemy had planned something huge.

Total obliteration, that's what Mr. Hitler wanted. Radar picked up a huge squadron of Luftwaffe Junkers over the coast. With Messerschmitt fighter planes acting as guard. There were so many that day the sky was black with them."

From the back of the classroom, Jack beamed with pride. The entire class was hanging on the old man's every word. For a moment he felt like the coolest kid in school.

"We had no time to lose. The enemy was coming in fast. If we didn't take to the air immediately, we would have been knocked out on the ground."

"Oh no," said an enraptured girl at the front.

"Oh yes!" continued Grandpa. "The whole airfield would have gone up in flames. My squadron was the first to be scrambled, and as Wing Commander I was to lead the charge. Within seconds we were all in the air. Up, up, and away. I pushed my Spitfire to three hundred miles an hour…"

"Wow!" said a boy at the back, looking up from his football magazine. "Three hundred miles an hour!"

"The Air Chief Marshal radioed me to tell me we would be outnumbered. He said four to one. So I had to think fast. We needed an element of surprise. I ordered my squadron to hide up above the clouds. The plan was we would wait until the enemy were so close we could smell them, and then

ATTACK!"

"So what date was this exactly, Mr. Bunting?" interrupted the teacher. "I need to put it up on the blackboard in red chalk. Red chalk is for dates only."

Miss Verity used strict color-coding on her blackboard:

Red chalk—dates

Green chalk—places

Blue chalk—events

Orange chalk—famous battles

Pink chalk—quotes

Purple chalk—kings and queens

Yellow chalk—politicians

White chalk—military leaders

Black chalk—doesn't show up well on a blackboard.
Use sparingly.

Grandpa thought for a moment. Jack's tummy twisted. He knew dates were not the old man's strong suit.

But eventually Grandpa replied confidently, "July the third, eleven hundred hours. I remember it well!"

The teacher wrote these **facts, facts, facts** up on the blackboard, the red chalk squeaking as Grandpa continued.

"So I waited until the very last moment. As soon as I saw the first Messerschmitt emerge from under the clouds, I gave the order.

DIVE!"

"What year was this?"

"Pardon me, madam?"

"What year was this?" Miss Verity pressed.

Then disaster. The old man's face went blanker than blank.

10

Facts, Facts, Facts

From the back of the classroom, Jack dived in to defend his grandfather. "Miss, it's best you don't keep on interrupting by asking questions…"

"But this is a history lesson! We need **facts! Facts! Facts!**" replied Miss Verity.

"Just please let the Wing Commander finish his story, miss, and we can get to all those later."

"Very well," muttered the history teacher, grasping her red chalk in readiness. "Please carry on, Mr. Bunting."

"Thank you, madam," said Grandpa. "Now, where was I?"

It was clear the poor old man had lost his thread. It was a good job that his grandson knew this story so well. He had heard this particular tale of derring-do hundreds of times but never tired of it. Jack prompted his grandfather. "You saw the first Messerschmitt, and gave the order to—"

"DIVE! That's right, man! As soon as my squadron of Spitfires descended through the clouds, we realized that this would be the fight of our lives." Grandpa's eyes lit up. He was back in the moment as if it were yesterday. "The radar had estimated a hundred planes in total. This looked more like two hundred! One hundred Junkers, and as many Messerschmitts. As for us, we had just twenty-seven Spitfires."

The children were enraptured. Miss Verity was busy scribbling up her precious **facts, facts, facts** on the blackboard—like how many aircraft on each side—in an array of multicolored chalks. As soon as she had finished, she switched back to red chalk (for dates only) and opened her mouth as if she were about to speak. But before she could say a word, the entire class went, **"SHUSH!"**

Grandpa was on a roll now. All the children were eating out of his hand. "I pressed on my machine guns and the battle commenced. It was thrilling and terrifying in equal measure. The sky was filled with bullets, smoke, and fire.

Bang!

I hit my first Messerschmitt. The Luftwaffe pilot parachuted out.

Bang!

And another!

"Our mission that day was to take down the Junkers. They were the deadly ones. Each one of those bombers was carrying tons of explosives. If we didn't stop them, their bombs would be raining down on the men, women, and children of London. Up in the skies, the battle raged for what seemed like hours. The RAF must have shot down fifty enemy aircraft that day," continued Grandpa. "Many of the other Luftwaffe planes were so badly damaged, they had to retreat back across the Channel quick smart. My squadron returned to base that day as heroes."

All the children in the class burst into wild applause.

"HOORAY!"

11

A Legend

As the applause died down in the classroom, Grandpa began again. "But this was no time for celebration. We knew the enemy would be back, and soon. In even greater numbers than before. The Battle of Britain had well and truly begun. As for my squadron, I lost four brave pilots that day."

The old man's eyes glistened with tears.

The entire class sat in stunned silence. So this was what a history lesson could be!

The boy sitting next to Jack turned to him and whispered, "Your grandpa is a legend!"

"I know," Jack replied, and smiled.

"Well, thank you so much for your time, Mr. Bunting," said Miss Verity loudly, breaking the spell.

"We are nearing the end of the lesson now. I have my red chalk poised at the ready. We need to note down all those **facts, facts, facts!** So please could you tell us all the year this happened?"

"The year?" replied Grandpa.

"Yes. I need to put it up on the board. If my pupils are to have any hope of passing their exam next term, we need to know **facts, facts, facts!** And yet more **facts**."

The old man looked at the teacher, confused. "It's this year."

"What do you mean this year?" asked the teacher.

"This year, madam. 1940."

The class chuckled uncertainly. Surely the old man was joking? Jack shifted uncomfortably in his seat.

Miss Verity gave everyone another of her famous death stares and they were silent once more. "You seriously think this is 1940?"

"Yes, of course it's 1940! King George VI is on the throne. And Mr. Churchill is the Prime Minister."

"No no no, Mr. Bunting. This is 1983!"

"It can't be!"

"Yes yes yes. Queen Elizabeth II is on the throne. And the wonderful Mrs. Thatcher is the Prime Minister."

Grandpa did not look at all convinced. In fact, he stared at the teacher as if she was **BONKERS!** "Mrs.?! A lady Prime Minister?! You must have a screw loose, madam!"

"I think it is *you* who has the screw loose, Mr. Bunting! Well, thank you so much for your oh-so-informative visit," said the teacher sarcastically. "Now, good-bye." As if shooing a pigeon, Miss Verity ushered the old man out of his chair. Under her breath she muttered to the class, "No need to write down a thing the old man said, after all! He doesn't know what year it is and he is still wearing his slippers!"

Poor Grandpa stood at the front of the class. He had been soaring in the sky; now he looked like he had crash-landed on the ground. Jack's heart ached for him.

The bell rang not a moment too soon. The boy had never been so relieved a lesson had ended.

Jack pushed past the other children to get to his grandfather as they all shambled out of the classroom. It had gone from being the best history class ever to the absolute worst.

Just as Jack reached Grandpa, Miss Verity called the boy back. "Jack? May I have a word, please?"

"A moment, sir," said the boy to his grandpa, as he plodded over to his teacher.

"Promise me you will never bring your grandfather into my classroom again," the lady hissed.

"I promise!" replied Jack angrily. "There's no way I am bringing him back here."

The boy spun around and reached out for Grandpa's hand. His old skin felt almost like a child's. Soft and silky.

"Come along, Wing Commander. Let's return to base."

"I don't... I don't understand," muttered the old man. "Was the briefing not clear? Did I let you down?"

Seeing his grandfather like this, it was hard not to cry. But Jack was determined to be strong. "No, Wing Commander, you didn't. You never have and you never will."

12

Bunking Off

Bunking off school was not something Jack had ever done before. However, he knew he had to make sure Grandpa got all the way home. The old man was much more confused than usual. Miss Verity had completely taken the wind from beneath his wings and now Grandpa was looking a little wobbly.

And the last thing the boy wanted to do was call his parents. If they found out how disastrously Grandpa's visit to the school had gone, chances were they would want to send him straight to Twilight Towers. So Jack led them back to Grandpa's flat.

When the pair approached, Raj was in the grimy window of his shop. The newsagent was busy showing off his artistic side. He was arranging a rather surreal display of his two main special offers for the

week—licorice and football cards. The licorice was wrapped around the cards, making both look highly undesirable. As soon as he spotted Jack and his grandfather, Raj rushed out of his shop to greet them.

"Ah! Mr. Bumting! Master Bumting!"

"It's Bunting!" corrected Jack.

"That's what I said!" protested Raj. "Bumting!"

Like all the local children, Jack liked the newsagent very much. The man never failed to put a smile on his face.

"So, Mr. Bumting, how is my favorite customer today? I was worried sick when you went missing from your flat in the middle of the night."

"Ah, Char Wallah! There you are!" proclaimed Grandpa.

"Char Wallah? What on earth does that mean?" asked Jack. He had never heard such a phrase before.

Raj whispered to the boy, "I asked my father back in India. He told me it's the name for an Indian man who serves tea—they sometimes did to British soldiers during World War II. I think your grandfather is getting more confused by the day."

"What's that, Char Wallah?" barked Grandpa, as he started helping himself to some out-of-date bars of chocolate.

"Nothing, sir!" replied Raj. "I've found it's much easier just to go along with him," he added in a whisper to Jack.

"Me too," replied the boy. "Now, I am going to need some help in getting him settled upstairs."

"Of course, young man. Before we go, might I be able to interest you in a copy of the *Radio Times* from 1975?"

"No, thank you, Raj."

The newsagent was not giving up. "Many of the shows on TV now are repeats, so it might still be accurate."

"We really should be getting him upstairs."

"Of course. Now what would you give me for this chocolate-covered toffee? Someone has licked off the chocolate and the toffee center is missing." With that the newsagent took out a shiny piece of purple paper from his pocket.

"Raj, that's just the wrapper!"

"That's why it's
half price."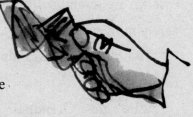

"There's no sweet!"

"You can sniff the
wrapper!"

"Enough chitter chatter, thank you, Char Wallah!"

interrupted Grandpa, as he stuffed a few of the out-of-date chocolate bars in his pockets for later. "It's time for my afternoon nap!"

It felt strange putting an old man to bed. Up until recently, it would have been Grandpa tucking Jack in. Now the roles had been reversed.

Of late, Grandpa would become tired during the day. So he took an hour's nap every day after lunch. Raj had locked up his shop for a short while so he could help Jack get his grandfather safely up the stairs.

"Forty winks!" That's what Grandpa always called his naptime. Raj drew the frayed curtains in the bedroom, as Jack arranged the old man's blanket.

"Make sure my Spitfire is full up with fuel, will you, Squadron Leader? I need to be at the ready in case we are scrambled! The Luftwaffe could be back at any moment."

"Yes, of course, Grandpa," replied Jack without thinking.

"Who's this 'Grandpa'?" he demanded, suddenly looking wide awake.

"I mean, yes, of course, *Wing Commander*, sir."
Jack added a salute to complete the illusion.

"That's better, Officer. Dismissed. I'm plum
tuckered out!"

With that, the boy's grandfather saluted and
stifled a yawn. As soon as he had closed his eyes, the
deafening snoring began.

"Zzzzzz! ZZzzzz! ZZZzzz! ZZZZzz!
ZZZZZz! ZZZZZZ!"

Up and down went the ends of the old man's
mustache as Jack and Raj tiptoed out of his bedroom.

13

The Willies

Back down in his newsagent's shop, Raj pulled out two old wooden crates for him and Jack to sit on. Next he rummaged around for something to eat, before deciding upon a battered Easter egg and half a packet of cheesy biscuits that had somehow found their way behind the radiator.

"Thank you so much for calling my dad last night, Raj," said Jack.

"Of course, young Master Bumting. If truth be told, it isn't the first time your grandfather has wandered out after dark."

"I know," replied the boy. His face clouded with worry. A man of his grandfather's age going missing at night in the depths of winter could one day be fatal.

"The times before, I had always managed to chase down the street after him and bring him back upstairs.

As you can see, I have an athletic build," said the newsagent, as he slapped his tummy. It wobbled like a huge jelly, and like an earthquake the aftershocks went on for quite a while. "But last night I just wasn't fast enough. I was feeling a little woozy as I had been at the chocolate liqueurs."

Jack wasn't sure you could actually get tipsy on them. "How many did you have, Raj?"

"Just three," replied the newsagent innocently.

"Surely there can't be much alcohol in just three?"

"Three boxes that is," confessed Raj. "I feel rather hungover today. You see I hadn't sold them at Christmas and they had gone out of date."

"But it's only January."

"This was Christmas 1979."

"Oh," replied the boy.

"They had gone white," the newsagent admitted. "Anyway, by the time I had finally managed to get out of bed, get dressed, and stumble out on to the street, he had gone. I chased up and down the road, but there was no sign of him. Your grandfather can move fast. His mind may be going, but his body is still strong. So I rushed back into my flat, flicked through the telephone directory, but there is a misprint as it says 'Bunting' and not 'Bumting.'"

The boy was about to interrupt to correct Raj, but thought better of it.

"Still, eventually I found the number and called your father. Mr. Bumting said he would go out and look for him in the car. Which reminds me, where on earth did you find your grandfather in the end?"

"We looked all over town, Raj," said Jack, picking up the story. "But we were looking in the wrong places. We were looking down when we should have been looking up."

The newsagent scratched his head. "I don't follow you," he said as he popped another cheesy biscuit in his mouth. "These are covered in furry mold," he added, before pouring them all down his throat.

"My grandpa always says 'Up, up, and away.' He used to say it during takeoff when he was a pilot with the RAF."

"So?"

"So, I knew he would be up high somewhere. Now, where do you think is the highest point in the town?"

Raj looked lost in thought for a moment. "That jar of Jelly Babies is very high up. I need a stepladder to get all the way up there."

Jack shook his head impatiently. "No! It's the church spire."

"Goodness gracious! How on earth did your grandfather get up there?"

"He must have climbed up. He wanted to touch the sky. When he was up there he thought he was piloting his Spitfire."

"Dear oh dear. On top of a church spire, thinking he's driving a plane? The old man is lucky to be alive. I fear your grandfather's mind is getting worse by the day."

The truth hit the boy like a runaway train and his eyes filled with tears. Instinctively Raj put his arm around the boy's shoulders. "There, there, Jack, it's OK to cry. Would you like to buy a pack of used tissues?"

Jack didn't fancy drying his eyes where a stranger had blown their nose, so he replied, "No, thank you, Raj. The thing is, my mum and dad want Grandpa to go into that new old folk's home, *Twilight Towers*."

"Oh dear," muttered Raj, shaking his head.

"What's the matter?"

"I am sorry, young Master Bumting, but I do not like the look of that place one bit. It gives me the **willies!**"

"It *is* on the edge of the moors."

Raj shuddered at the thought. "Some local people say the only way out of *Twilight Towers* is in a coffin," he added gravely.

"No!" exclaimed Jack. "Well, he can't go there. But, Raj—my parents have made up their minds. They are set on it!"

"Why can't your grandfather come and live with your family?"

Suddenly a broad smile lit up the boy's face. "I'd love that!"

"That's how we do things in India! The old folk are looked after by the younger folk. I have my elderly aunt living up in the flat with me."

"I didn't know that."

"Yes, Auntie Dhriti. She can't actually leave the flat."

"Is she too old?"

"No. Too big." His voice lowered, and he looked up at the ceiling. "She was always a large lady, but since living above a sweet shop she has **ballOOned**. I would have to hire a crane and knock down a wall if she ever wanted to pop out."

Jack painted this image in his mind for a moment—a large lady in a brightly colored sari being

winched out across the street. Then his thoughts returned to the important matter at hand: his grandfather.

"We don't have a spare room, but I've got bunk beds. In fact, Grandpa stayed last night. There's no reason why he can't stay forever! Raj, you are a genius!"

"I know," replied the newsagent.

"I am going to run home and tell my mum and dad right away."

"You do that, young Master Bumting!"

The boy dashed toward the door.

"And please tell your good parents to pop by my shop soon. I have an excellent deal going on yogurt. Well, I say yogurt, it's last month's milk and…"

But before the newsagent could finish his sentence, the boy was gone.

14

Cartwheels of Joy

Needless to say, Jack's parents had been extremely reluctant to move the old man into their home. However, the boy made such a passionate case for his grandfather that they finally caved in. Grandpa wouldn't take up any space, because he would sleep in the boy's bedroom. Plus Jack promised he would look after him whenever he was not at school. When his parents finally said yes, the boy wanted to cartwheel up and down the living room his heart was so full of joy.

"This is only for a trial period," Jack's mother reminded him.

"We are not sure we can cope forever, either, son," muttered Dad sadly. "The doctors said his condition will get a lot worse over time. I don't want you to be disappointed if it doesn't work out."

"And if he goes missing in the night again," announced Mum, "then that's it, Jack! He has to go straight to Twilight Towers!"

"Of course! Of course! He'll be sleeping in my bedroom, so I can make sure that will never happen!" exclaimed the boy. Then Jack raced out of the house back to Grandpa's flat to tell him the FANTASTIC news, grinning all the way.

15

Snoring Like an Elephant

Jack helped the old man pack up all his belongings from his little flat. Aside from his memories, Grandpa didn't have much. Flying goggles, a pot of mustache wax, a tin of spam. Then they walked the short distance to Grandpa's new "quarters."

As soon as they were upstairs in the boy's bedroom, the pair were playing World War II pilots. They were meant to have been in bed hours ago. However, together they took to the skies, Grandpa in his beloved Spitfire and Jack in his speedy Hurricane. "Up, *up, and away!*" they cried, as they battled the mighty Luftwaffe. They made such a racket, they were in danger of waking up the whole street. For a moment, Jack didn't care that he had no close friends to invite over to stay. This was the best sleepover ever! Just as the pair of flying aces were bringing their imaginary planes in to land, Mum thumped on the bedroom door. She shouted, "I said, 'LIGHTS OUT!'"

"I do wish that blasted charlady would keep it down!" said Grandpa.

"I HEARD THAT!" came the woman's voice from the other side of the door.

After a game of cards in the "officers' mess" by torchlight, the old man made his way over to the bedroom window. He looked up at the empty sky. Only a faint sprinkling of stars could be seen twinkling through the dark.

"What are you doing, sir?" asked the boy.

"I am listening for enemy aircraft, old boy."

"Can you hear any?" said Jack excitedly. He was

now sat cross-legged on the top bunk, his model planes dangling around his head.

"Shush..." shushed Grandpa. "Sometimes the Luftwaffe pilots switch off their engines and just let their planes glide. The enemy's chief weapon is surprise. All that gives them away is the sound of the wind whistling past the wings. Listen..."

Jack cleared his mind of thoughts and concentrated hard on listening. It was absurd, if you thought about it. Here they were in 1983, listening out for planes that hadn't flown over the British Isles for nearly half a century. But it was so real in Grandpa's mind, Jack couldn't help but believe it too.

"They would have been here by now, if they were coming tonight. We must doss down for the night. There is every chance the enemy are planning a dawn bombing raid."

"Yes, Wing Commander," said Jack, saluting his grandfather, not sure whether bedtime was the appropriate time to salute.

Grandpa closed the window, and shuffled over to the bottom bunk. "Well, good night, old boy," he said as he turned out the light. "I hope you don't snore. I can't abide snorers!"

With that, the old man fell instantly asleep and started snoring as loudly as a bull elephant. "ZZZZZ… ZZZZZ ZZZZZZZZZZZZ." The ends of his mustache fluttered like a butterfly's wings.

Jack lay there on the top bunk, wide awake. Despite the deafening sound of the snoring, he couldn't be happier. He had saved his grandfather from being sent to Twilight Towers. Now that the whole family was under one roof, the boy had a warm fuzzy feeling in his tummy.

Jack's head rested on his pillow. Underneath it he had hidden the key to his room. The boy had promised his parents that the old man wouldn't go walkies in  the middle of the night again, so while Grandpa was looking the other way he had locked the bedroom door.

The boy stared up at his model planes, spinning in the dark. *If only they were real*, he thought. Jack closed his eyes and began imagining he was in the cockpit of a World War II fighter plane, flying high above the clouds. Before long he was fast asleep.

16

Empty Bunk

DDDRRRIIINGGG!!!

The next thing Jack knew, his alarm was going off, as it did every weekday morning at seven o'clock. As he lay on the top bunk in his bedroom, his hand groped for his old tin wind-up RAF clock, and he turned it off. With his eyes still closed, the boy suddenly remembered that his grandfather had gone to sleep on the bottom bunk. He lay there for a moment, listening out for the old man's snoring. *That's strange*, thought Jack. He couldn't hear a thing. Yet he could feel the key still safely hidden under his pillow. The door must still be locked. There was no way Grandpa could have gotten out.

All of a sudden Jack realized he was cold. Painfully cold. The top of his blanket felt icy. The model planes above his head were lightly dusted with frost. It had to be the same temperature inside as it was out.

At that moment the winter wind whipped up… making his curtains flap. The window must be open! For a moment Jack couldn't bear to look below to the bottom bunk. Slowly he summoned all his courage. He took a deep breath, before peeping down.

The bottom bunk was empty.

The bed was so neatly made, it was as if it had never been slept in. That was very Grandpa. Despite making a daring escape in the middle of the night, he couldn't leave the bed unmade. His time in the RAF had made him a stickler for everything being spick and span.

Leaping down from the bunk bed, Jack dashed to the window. He looked along the row of frosted gardens for some sign of the old man. Next his eyes searched all the trees, roofs, and even lampposts, in case his grandfather had climbed up one of them. Nothing. Beyond the gardens sat the park. It was still early and empty of people. The wide expanse of grass was covered with a thick layer of frost and Jack couldn't make out any footprints.

Grandpa was long gone.

17

Nothing

Days and nights went by with no sign of the old man. The townsfolk formed search parties, the police were called out, and Jack even made a tearful appeal for his safe return on the local news.

Nothing.

On the boy's instruction, all the highest points for miles around were checked. The tops of hills, roofs of any tall buildings, the church spire of course, even electricity pylons.

Nothing.

Jack designed a Missing poster for his grandfather. He had hundreds photocopied at school and trundled around town on his trike, sticking them up on every tree and lamppost he could find.

Nothing.

Every time the telephone or the doorbell rang, Jack would race to answer it, praying it would be news about Grandpa. But there was no trace of him.

The boy felt terribly guilty and would cry himself to sleep at night. His mum and dad told Jack not to blame himself, but over and over he wished that he had listened to them.

Perhaps an old folk's home really was the best place for Grandpa? At least he would be safe there. Though the boy hated to admit it, it seemed Grandpa was now far too much of a handful for the family to look after.

As each day passed, the sense of absence grew deeper.

Yet after a while, Jack realized something awful. The world kept turning; his mum and dad went back to work. The people of the town returned to their lives. A missing old man had become old news.

Most of all, it was the not knowing that was agonizing. Had Grandpa gone forever? Or was he lost somewhere, in desperate need of help?

Reluctantly the boy returned to school. It was hard to concentrate at the best of times, but now Jack's mind really was elsewhere. Whatever the subject, all he could think about was his grandpa.

After school every day he would stop off at Raj's shop to see if there was any news.

DING! went the bell as Jack

entered the newsagent's. It was now a whole week after his grandfather's disappearance.

"Ah! Young Master Bumting! My favorite customer! Come in out of the cold, please!" called Raj from behind his counter.

In such a low mood, all the boy could muster was a polite nod in the newsagent's direction.

"I scoured all the newspapers again today, but I am sorry to say there has been no sign of your grandfather," said Raj.

"I just don't understand!" replied Jack. "When he went missing before we always found him. This time it's like he's disappeared into thin air."

Raj mused on this thought for a while, and to aid

concentration picked up a lolly from the counter and popped it in his mouth. The man's face grimaced a little, it was clear he didn't like the taste, and he quickly popped it back with the others for sale.

There had long been rumors among the kids at Jack's school that many of Raj's sweets came "presucked." Now the boy knew for sure. Strangely, it didn't make him like the newsagent any less.

"Your grandfather is a war hero…" said Raj, thinking out loud.

"Yes! He even has a Distinguished Flying Cross!" agreed Jack. "That's one of the highest honors a pilot could be awarded."

"…So I cannot believe a man like that would just give up on life. He's out there somewhere. I just know it."

DING! The boy left the shop with a spring in his step for the first time in days. Now at least Jack felt there was hope. The drone of an airplane's engine echoed across the sky. Looking up, for a moment Jack half expected to see his grandfather. But of course it wasn't a Spitfire. Just another anonymous jumbo jet.

"Up, *up,* and away," the boy recited to himself.

Raj was right—Grandpa must be out there.

But where?

18

Jiggery-Pokery

Day trips were something of a rarity at Jack's school. After a boy had slid down the *Tyrannosaurus rex* skeleton at the Natural History Museum on his bottom, the headmaster had banned all trips until further notice. It was only one of a long list of misdeeds committed by pupils at Jack's school over the years. Most had now entered into school legend…

– At London Zoo, a girl leaped over the wall at the penguin enclosure. She thought that by tugging her pullover over her head, and waddling and catching a fish in her mouth, she could pass herself off as a penguin.

– A trip to a Doctor Who exhibition ended in chaos when a number of boys stole Cybermen, Sontaran, and Dalek costumes and pretended that there was an alien invasion of Earth.

– One Christmas, on a school outing to see the local pantomime, two pupils stole the pantomime horse costume. They were only found out when several months later they attempted to enter the Grand National.

– An excursion to an ancient fort took an unfortunate turn when the teacher was fired out of a cannon. He was later found up a tree two miles away.

– On an outing to the HMS *Victory*, a group of boys pulled up the anchor and set sail. They hoisted a skull-and-crossbones flag and declared that they were pirates. After several months at sea, the boys were apprehended by a Royal Navy aircraft carrier.

– A day trip to a local farm ended in disaster when the geography teacher was herded into a sheep dip and all his hair was sheared off. It was slightly preferable to the previous year, when the pupils had attached him to the milking machine.

– At the National Gallery a boy scrawled "Gaz Woz Ere" with a black marker pen on a priceless Turner masterpiece. At first he denied it, before being reminded that he was the only boy in the school called Gaz.

– An outing to the Bank of England ended in disgrace for the school when they realized £1,000,000 had gone missing. The maths teacher Mr. Filch is still in prison for his role in the robbery.

– On a visit to the local fire station the fire chief regretted letting the children loose on one of the hoses. A teacher was propelled into the air by the spray and kept up there for over an hour until the water ran out.

– The school had been banned forever from Madame Tussaud's waxworks in London after a couple of boys made off with the replica of Mrs. Thatcher. The next day they wheeled the waxwork around the school on a skateboard, pretending the Prime Minister was on a visit.

Despite this long list of offences, Miss Verity petitioned the headmaster to lift the ban. Eventually she was granted permission to take her history class on a visit to the Imperial War Museum in London.

Miss Verity was well-known for being the strictest teacher in the school and the headmaster was sure there would be no funny business on her watch.

Jack had been so distracted by his grandfather's being missing, he had all but forgotten about the trip. First thing in the morning, and with his head elsewhere, the boy boarded the coach. Needless to say, before the coach had even left the playground, all the kids had scoffed the entire contents of their packed lunch boxes. The greedy little tykes.

Returning to the Imperial War Museum was bittersweet for the boy. Jack had visited it so many times before with Grandpa, it was like a second home to them. Of course, this was when his grandfather still knew he was his grandfather.

As the coach pulled up outside, Jack recognized the museum at once. It was an impressive building, with Roman-style columns at the front, a green dome on the roof, and the two naval cannon pointing proudly aloft in the courtyard.

The trip was nearly canceled before anyone had even got off the coach. Two boys on the backseat had pushed their bottoms against the window to moon some elderly Japanese tourists. After Miss Verity gave them both life sentences in detention, she made a speech to all the children on the coach.

"Now, listen up!" she shouted over the excited hum. The children were buzzing, having wolfed down all the cakes and chocolate bars in their lunch boxes. They were far too hyper to be quiet. "I said LISTEN UP!" she bellowed. And there was silence. "Every single one of you will be on your best behavior today. You are all a walking advertisement for the school. If there is even a hint of *jiggery-pokery*, **monkey business**, or shenanigans of any kind, we are all getting straight back on the coach."

Like all the other kids, Jack had no idea what "jiggery-pokery" meant exactly. But he imagined it might include sliding down a priceless dinosaur skeleton on your bottom.

"Now, here are your worksheets!" announced Miss Verity, handing out bundles of A4 paper. There was an audible groan from all the kids, who were looking forward to the day trip being something of a "doss." "There's even a sheet for you," she said, as she handed one to the baffled-looking coach driver. "What I am looking for today are the three

F's. Facts. Facts. Facts."

Jack scanned his worksheet. There were hundreds of questions, all dealing with boring historical details. Dates, names, places. Jack and his classmates were going to have no time to marvel at the exhibits. Instead, they'd have to spend the entire time reading every sign on every wall and jotting down every last **fact, fact, fact**.

The Imperial War Museum was full from floor to ceiling with tanks, weaponry, and uniforms, all from

past and present. Jack's favorite part of the museum was the Great Room, where planes hung from the ceiling. It had inspired him to display his model airplanes in his bedroom in much the same way.

The museum had the most remarkable collection of fighter planes. There was a World War I biplane, the Sopwith Camel, a Luftwaffe Focke-Wulf, and an American Mustang. However, pride of place was given to the most legendary fighter plane of them all. The Spitfire.

On seeing her again, Jack's heart began to sing. Somehow she made the boy feel close to his grandpa again.

19

Bird of Prey

Most of the kids from Jack's school wanted to race through the Imperial War Museum as fast as they could. Their plan was to head straight to the gift shop and spend their pocket money on something completely unrelated to the exhibits. Like a smelly eraser in the shape of an ice cream that they could sniff all the way home.

All Jack wanted to do was stare at the Spitfire. The machine always had this pull on him. Today that pull seemed stronger than ever. The Spitfire had been built to bring death and destruction, but she was also a thing of great beauty. Seeing her again, Jack understood why this particular fighter plane, above all others, had entered into legend.

If only he could take to the air. *"Up, up, and away,"* he muttered to himself. It seemed a shame that this great warbird was gathering dust in a museum, when she should be ZOOMING through the sky.

From every angle the Spitfire was stunning. Looking at her from below, Jack noticed how her underneath was as smooth and pale as the underside of a killer whale. The wings appeared strong and powerful, like those of a bird of prey. Jack's most favorite part of all was the wooden propeller. Sat on the nose of the plane, it looked more like a military mustache. It was as if the Spitfire wasn't a machine at all, but a person.

In this tall display room there were flights of steps that led up to a raised walkway. This gave visitors a better look at all the different planes dangling from the ceiling. But when Jack went up there to study the Spitfire further, he noticed something very curious. The Perspex bubble that sat atop the Spitfire cockpit had steamed up. There had to be something heating it from the inside.

Yet more curious was the sound coming from the cockpit. It was the sound of snoring.

Zzzzzz! Zzzzzzzz! Zzzzzzzz!

Someone must be fast asleep in the Spitfire!

20

Breaking the Rules

"Come along, Jack!" called out Miss Verity from below, before turning to go into the next room of the museum.

"Coming, miss!" the boy shouted down from the walkway, even though he had no intention of following her just yet. He needed to find out if someone really was asleep in the Spitfire.

"Hello?" called Jack now in the direction of the fighter plane.

ZZZZZZZZZZZzzz!
ZZZZzzZ!

There was no response.

"HELLO!" he called out again, a little louder this time.

ZZZZZZZZZZZZzzz
ZZZZZZZZZZZzzz!

ZZZZZZZZZZZzzz
ZZZZZZZZZZZZzzz
ZZZZZZZZZZZZzz!

Still no response.

From the walkway it was impossible for the boy to reach the Spitfire directly. A running jump was sure to be fatal. The planes were all suspended high off the ground.

However, the wing of the Sopwith Camel was not far from the walkway. If Jack could somehow clamber on to that, then he would be able to crawl along it on to the next plane. Eventually he would be able to reach the Spitfire.

Jack could be brave in his imaginary airplane. But he had never felt brave in real life, just shy and rather timid. Now he was about to break all the rules.

Jack took a deep breath. Not daring to look down, the boy climbed up on to the handrail of the walkway. He closed his eyes for a moment before leaping on to the wing of the World War I biplane.

THUNK!

The Sopwith Camel was largely made of wood and much lighter than the boy had imagined. His weight made the ancient fighter plane wobble. For a moment Jack was terrified he might lose his balance and plummet to the ground. Thinking fast, he crouched down to his hands and knees to spread his weight. Scuttling like a crab he moved along the wings until he was near the next plane.

This was the Luftwaffe's dreaded Focke-Wulf. To reach it, the boy had to make a jump.

Once again, he took a deep breath and sprang through the air.

THUNK!

He landed on the wing of the Focke-Wulf. Now Jack was just one plane away from the Spitfire. The boy was so close the snoring coming from the cockpit was extremely loud.

ZZZZZZZZZZZzz
zzZZZZZZZZZzz
ZZZZZZZZZZZzz!

Unless it really was a bull elephant asleep up there, he knew that snoring only too well…

21

Jungle Roar

"OI! YOU!" The shout rang through the Great Room.

Jack gulped and looked down from the wing of the Luftwaffe Focke-Wulf. He had never really been in trouble before. Now here he was in the Imperial War Museum, leaping from wing to wing of priceless antique fighter planes.

An extremely large security guard was looking up at him. It was like the museum had captured the biggest gorilla in the jungle, stuffed it into a uniform and placed a peaked cap on its head. Thick tufts of black hair sprouted from his nose, neck and ears.

"ME?" asked the boy innocently, as if it was perfectly normal to be crouched on the wing of a World War II fighter plane hanging from the ceiling of the Imperial War Museum.

"YES! YOU! GET DOWN FROM THERE!"

"Now?" said Jack, still pretending he didn't know what all the fuss could be about.

"YES!" The man was becoming angry, his voice morphing into something of a jungle roar.

This roar was so loud that it drew all the museum's other visitors back into the room. Soon the children from Jack's school were looking up at their classmate in disbelief. The boy's face turned scarlet with embarrassment. Finally Miss Verity herself stormed in, her long flowing skirt swishing along the floor.

"Jack Bunting!" she fumed. You knew you were in trouble when a teacher used your full name. "Come down from there this instant. You are bringing disgrace on the school!"

The school had a very poor reputation, so Jack wasn't sure he could bring further disgrace upon it. However, this was not the time or place to argue.

What's more, the boy had more important things on his mind. "I just need to jump on to this Spitfire, miss, then I promise I'll come straight down!" he said.

There was a ripple of laughter from all the kids. The towering security guard did not find it funny. He bounded up on to the walkway. Not only did he *look* like a gorilla, he seemed to have the skills of one too. Soon he had leaped on to the wing of the Sopwith Camel. But also like a gorilla, he must have been ten times heavier than the boy. The biplane swung violently from side to side, its wing smashing into the next plane.

CRASH!!

This made the Focke-Wulf Jack was crouched on sway dramatically to the side.

SWING!

The poor boy lost his balance completely now. He stumbled, dropped and was left hanging from the Focke-Wulf's wing by his fingertips.

"Argh!"

Jack cried in fear.
"Hold on, Jack!"
cried Miss Verity from below. The Great Room at the Imperial War Museum

had never seen such drama. "It would reflect badly on me if a pupil was to lose their life on a school trip."

Jack could feel his fingers slipping off the cold shiny metal of the Focke-Wulf's wing, one by one.

"STAY RIGHT THERE!"

growled the security guard.

What else am I going to do? thought the boy.

It was an awfully

long

      way

         d

           o

             w

                n.

22

Forty Winks

Just at that moment, Jack spied the cockpit of the Spitfire sliding open.

"What's all this noise? Can't a pilot catch forty winks in peace?!"

"Grandpa!" shouted the boy in joy that he had found him at last.

"Who's this 'Grandpa'?" asked Grandpa. These days he never answered to that name, but sometimes it was easy to forget.

"Wing Commander!" Jack corrected himself.

"That's better!" said the old man as he climbed out of the cockpit and stood on the wing of the Spitfire. Grandpa looked down and saw he was suspended high above the ground. "Silly me! I must still be flying!" he muttered to himself, before turning to go back into the cockpit.

"No, you're not still flying, sir!" corrected the boy.

Jack's grandfather peered down at the growing crowd below. "This is most queer."

"Erm? Wing Commander?" said the boy, desperately trying to get his grandfather's attention.

Grandpa looked in the direction of Jack's voice. The boy was hanging by the tips of his fingers. "Squadron Leader, what on earth are you doing down there? Let me help you, old boy."

Grandpa shuffled along the Spitfire's wing to where Jack was dangling from the Focke-Wulf. The old man grabbed his grandson's hand. Despite being elderly, he

was surprisingly strong. On the other hand, sport was not Jack's strong suit, so he was grateful for the help.

In one go, Grandpa heaved the boy up on to the Spitfire's wing.

Whoops, cheers, and applause broke out among all the children on the ground.

Without thinking, Jack wrapped his arms around his grandfather and gave him a big hug. The old man had gone missing over a week ago, and Jack had thought he might never see him again.

"Remember there's a war on, Squadron Leader!" said Grandpa. Gently he unpeeled the boy's hands from around his waist, and they stood opposite each other and saluted.

Suddenly from behind them came a growl. **"YOU ARE IN BIG TROUBLE!"** It was the security guard.

Just at that moment the half man/half gorilla took a running jump from the Focke-Wulf on to the

Spitfire's wing. The weight of all three of them caused the cable above them to tighten and stretch.

Twang!

EEK!

Then finally...

SNap!

The Spitfire's wing swung down toward the ground; the plane now hung there with just one cable supporting it.

The three figures slid down the wing as the crowd below gasped.

Grandpa just managed to seize hold of the plane's propeller. Jack just managed to grab on to the old man's slippers. In turn, the security guard grabbed on to the boy's ankles and they all swung from side to side like a trapeze act.

THIS WAY UP

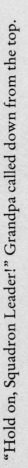

"Hold on, Squadron Leader!" Grandpa called down from the top.

"You hold on, Wing Commander!" the boy called up.

Below them they could hear someone sobbing. **"I DON'T WANT TO DIE!"** blubbed the security guard, choking back a river of tears.

"Look down!" said Miss Verity calmly.

"I'M TOO SCARED!"

he wailed, his voice cracking with terror. The security guard screwed up his eyes as tight as they could go.

"For goodness' sake, you are about an inch off the ground," sighed the teacher.

Slowly the guard opened his eyes and looked down. Being at the bottom of the human chain his boots were all but scuffing the ground.

"Oh!" he said, suddenly rather embarrassed that a large group of schoolchildren had seen him reduced to a blubbering mess. He counted to three, then let go of Jack's ankles. He dropped down the smallest distance to the floor.

The man turned to the teacher. "You saved my life," he choked, as he gave Miss Verity the most enormous bear hug and lifted her clean off the ground.

"My spectacles are getting squashed!" she protested. The whole situation made her look distinctly uncomfortable. This was especially true when she caught the eyes of the schoolkids, all giggling at their rather proper teacher in an embrace with a man.

"What about us?" Jack called down, still holding on to his grandfather's ankles.

"I will catch you!" said the security guard, in an attempt to regain his macho image. "Let go in three. One, two, three…"

"Righty ho!" said Grandpa.

Before the security guard could say anything, the old man had let go too.

Within the blink of an eye, Jack and then his grandfather landed on top of the guard, his huge body providing a perfect crash mat.

BOING!

Having two people fall on top of him knocked him out. The security guard was now lying flat on his back on the floor of the museum.

"Stand back, everyone!" ordered the teacher. "I need to give him the kiss of life!"

With that Miss Verity bent down to breathe air into the security guard's lungs. The man was just dazed, and soon came to.

"Thank you, Miss…?" said the security guard.

"Verity. But you can call me Veronica."

"Thank you, Veronica." The pair smiled at each other.

Then looking up, Miss Verity recognized Grandpa. "Oh, it's you again, Mr. Bunting! I should have known!"

With the security guard lying on the floor and a priceless antique Spitfire swinging from the ceiling, Jack thought it best to act as if absolutely nothing had happened.

"So that's the Battle of Britain covered, Miss Verity," said the boy in a jolly tone. "What's next?"

"Next…" fumed the history teacher, "I am calling the police!"

23

Nuts and Berries

Like most children, Jack had always wanted a ride in a police car. However, he had always imagined he would be sitting up front, chasing baddies. Not in the back with a close family member who had just been put under arrest.

The police car raced through London with its siren **BLARING.** They were being taken to Scotland Yard for questioning, although Grandpa seemed to think he had been captured by "the enemy." The charge against the old man was "criminal damage." The boy had tried to explain to the policeman that if the security guard had not been quite so heavy, the cable suspending the Spitfire would never have snapped. Needless to say, this did not get his grandfather off the hook. The policeman was a very serious-looking character. He sat at the steering wheel not uttering a word for the entire journey to police headquarters.

As they were seated side by side in the backseat of the police car, Jack turned to his grandfather.

"Gran—I mean Wing Commander?"

"Yes, old boy?"

"How did you come to be asleep in the cockpit of your plane?" In all the excitement, Jack had quite forgotten to ask.

Grandpa looked stumped for a moment. He had been missing for a week. The Imperial War Museum was many miles away from home.

"It all started when I parachuted behind enemy lines…," began Grandpa eventually. It was clear that the old man was mightily confused and trying to bind together the events of the past week.

That must be his memory of jumping out of the bedroom window at home, thought the boy.

"I walked for many days and nights," Grandpa continued. "I kept off the main roads, stuck to the fields and woodland as much as I could. Just as we RAF pilots are trained to do if we are in occupied territory."

That's why no one saw him, thought Jack.

The boy looked down at his grandfather's slippers; they were caked with mud and looked soaked through. "But how did you survive?" asked Jack.

"I ate nuts and berries, and drank rainwater."

"And you slept under the stars?"

"The only way to sleep, Squadron Leader! Surely you have during your time in the RAF?" asked the old man.

Jack felt ashamed to reply, "No. Never." His grandfather's life had been a hundred times more exciting than his would ever be. "But how did you know where you were going?"

"I must have crossed the border into Allied territory, because from a field I saw this giant sign on a main road."

"What was on the sign?" asked Jack.

"A great big picture of a Spitfire! With directions no less! Most queer."

A billboard for the Imperial War Museum! realized the boy.

"I must get the Air Chief Marshal on the blower about that. Massive giveaway to the enemy where the nearest RAF base is. If they do manage to land ground troops, they can follow the directions and march straight there!"

The boy couldn't help but smile. Everyone else always saw Grandpa's condition as a problem. For Jack, the way his grandfather's mind worked was nothing short of magical.

"It was getting dark when I finally arrived at the air base," continued the old man. "And there were a few little blighters looking around the aircraft hangar—they must have been evacuees…"

The Imperial War Museum was always full of children. *This must be what he meant*, thought Jack.

"…I needed to use the bathroom. I hadn't been for a week. And all those nuts and berries make you go! But I was so tired, I must have fallen asleep on it. Just forty winks. When I woke up, someone had turned off all the lights. I wandered around in the dark for ages, but eventually managed to find my Spitfire. Had to clamber over some other planes to get to her, mind."

Grandpa was lucky to be alive! Climbing over all those antique planes suspended high in the air was dangerous enough with the lights on.

"And then what happened, sir?" Jack asked, intrigued.

"Then I thought I would take her for a spin. *Up, up, and away* and all that. Couldn't start the old girl! Must have been out of fuel…" Grandpa's voice trailed off, and a mystified look crossed his face. "Then… then… I suppose I must have fallen asleep again in the cockpit. Just another quick forty winks, you understand."

"Yes, of course, Wing Commander."

The pair sat in silence for a moment, before the boy broke it. A wave of love for his grandfather crashed over him. "You know everyone was really worried about you…"

Grandpa snorted at the thought. "No need to worry about me, old boy." He chuckled. "The whole of Mr. Hitler's Luftwaffe can't stop me. Oh no! This old pilot will always live to fight another day!"

24

A Wardrobe in a Suit

At Scotland Yard confusion reigned. None of the officers at the police headquarters had a clue what to do with this funny old man who had climbed into an airplane at the Imperial War Museum.

However, the charge was a serious one. Criminal damage. Because of the chaos at the museum earlier that day, three antique fighter planes were now in need of expensive repairs. So Grandpa was taken down into the basement of Scotland Yard to an interrogation room. Jack begged the officers to allow him to come too. The boy explained that his grandfather's mind could get jumbled up and that the old man would need his help. He wondered what on earth was going to happen next to his grandfather. A trial? Prison? The boy knew Grandpa was in trouble. The question was, how deep?

The interrogation room was small and dark, and everything in it was gray. The walls. The table. The chairs. A bare lightbulb hung down from the ceiling. There were no windows, just a small slit at the top of the door through which those outside could look in.

They had been sitting there alone for a while when four eyes appeared at the viewing slit.

Keys jangled and the huge metal door swung open. Two plainclothed police detectives stood in the doorway. It was time for the interrogation to begin.

One of the detectives was an unusually tall, broad man; a wardrobe in a suit. In contrast, his crime-fighting partner was stick thin. From a distance, you might have mistaken him for a snooker cue.

Down in the depths of Scotland Yard, both men tried to come through the doorway of the interview room at the same time. Needless to say, they became wedged in, their ill-fitting shiny gray suits rubbing up against each other.

"I am stuck!" called out the big man, Detective Beef.

"It's not my fault, *Kimberly*," said the thin man, Detective Bone.

"Don't call me *Kimberly* in front of the suspect!" Beef whispered loudly.

"But, *Kimberly* Beef, *Kimberly's* your name!"

"Stop saying it!"

"Sorry, *Kimberly*! I won't call you *Kimberly* ever again, *Kimberly*. That's a promise, *Kimberly*!"

"You keep saying it!"

It was obvious the bigger man hated having a girly name. No doubt he longed for something more butch like Chad or Kurt or Brad or Rock or Zeus or indeed Butch.

Eventually **Kimberly** managed to force himself through the doorway, squashing his counterpart in the process.

"You're hurting me!" cried Bone.

"Sorry!" said Beef.

Jack had to suppress a giggle as the pair stumbled into the room. In all the rumpus, they left the door wide-open with the chain of keys still stuck in it.

"Gestapo!" hissed Grandpa to his grandson. "Let me handle them!"

The Gestapo were Hitler's feared secret police force, a world away from these two clowns.

But when Grandpa became convinced of something, he would not let go, so Jack kept quiet.

Once the two detectives had brushed themselves off and straightened their ties, this un–dynamic duo took their seats opposite Jack and his grandfather.

There was an awkward silence for a long moment. Both detectives looked like they were waiting for the other to speak.

"Aren't you going to say something?" whispered Beef eventually out of the corner of his wide mouth.

"I thought we agreed that

you were going to speak first,"
replied Bone.

"Oh, yes, we did. Sorry."
There followed a pause. "But
now I don't know what to say."

"Excuse us a
moment," apologized Bone. The
two detectives gave Jack and his
grandfather embarrassed smiles
before stepping away from the
table once more. Jack was finding
this hilarious but didn't dare show it, while Grandpa's
face was a picture of bemusement.

In the corner of the small gray room the two
detectives huddled together, like rugby players
discussing tactics. Bone gave the orders to Beef.

"Look, **Kimberly**, we've
been through this before. We
do the good-cop, bad-cop
routine. It always breaks
them in the end."

"Yes!"

"Great!"

Beef thought for a moment. "Which one am I again?"

"The good cop!" Bone was becoming quite agitated now.

"But I want to be the bad cop," protested Beef. He was definitely the more childish of the two.

"I'm ALWAYS the bad cop!" said Bone.

"Not fair!" wailed Beef, acting as if a bigger boy had stolen his ice cream.

"All right, all right!" conceded Bone. "You can be the bad cop!"

"YES!" Beef punched the air in triumph.

"But only for today."

Jack was starting to feel impatient and called over from the table, "Sorry, are you going to be long?"

"No no no. We won't be a moment now," replied Bone, before turning back to his crime-fighting partner. "All right, I'll go first. As the good cop, I'll say something nice and then as the bad cop, you say something nasty."

"Got it!" replied Beef.

With confident strides the two detectives returned to their seats. The thin man spoke first.

"As you know, criminal damage is a serious charge. But you must remember that we are your friends. We are here to help you. We just need some answers as to what you were up to with those old fighter planes?"

"Yes," chipped in Beef. "If you would be so kind."

Detective Bone **groaned** in despair.

25

Deeper Doo-Doo

Things were not going to plan in the interview room. Detective Bone dragged Detective Beef back to the corner. "You fool! You are meant to be the bad cop! You can't just say, 'If you would be so kind.'"

"No?" asked Beef innocently.

"NO! You have to be menacing."

"Menacing?"

"YES!"

"I am not sure I can be menacing. It's hard to be menacing with a name like *Kimberly*."

"I don't think they know that's your name."

"You've said it a hundred times!" exclaimed Beef.

"Oh yes. Sorry, *Kimberly*," replied Bone.

"You just did it again!"

"Apologies, *Kimberly*."

"And again!"

"I promise it won't happen again, *Kimberly*."

"Please stop saying my name! Maybe it's best that I am the good cop, after all."

"But you just said you wanted to be the bad cop!"

"I know…" Beef looked very sheepish. "But I have decided I would like to swap. If you would be so kind."

Bone hastily agreed. The interrogation was fast turning into a farce. "All right, all right. Have it your way. You be the good cop, *Kimberly*, and I'll be the bad cop."

"Thank you. And remember, please don't call me *Kimberly* in front of the suspect."

"Sorry, did I call you *Kimberly* again?"

"Yes, you did," declared Beef.

"Sorry, *Kimberly*," replied Bone.

Jack couldn't help himself any longer and a laugh leaped out of his mouth.

"Ha-ha!"

"What's so funny?" demanded Beef angrily.

"Nothing, *Kimberly*!" snickered the boy.

Kimberly looked as furious as someone called *Kimberly* could look. "Now they know my name is *Kimberly*! And it's all your fault!"

Bone was not ready to accept all the blame. "I think your mother and father are most at fault really, naming you '*Kimberly* Beef' in the first place. Why on earth would they give you a girl's name?!"

"*Kimberly* is not a girl's name!" Beef shouted. "It's unisex!"

Other supposedly "unisex" names Mr. and Mrs. Beef could have called their bouncing baby boy include

Alice
Carol
Darryl
Hayley
Jordan
Lindsay
Marion
Meredith
Paris
Sandy
Stacy
Or Tracy

"Oh yes, of course it's a unisex name, you meet so many men called **Kimberly**," muttered Detective Bone, before composing himself. "Now look, we

have an interrogation to do, remember?"

"Yes. Yes. Sorry."

"And remember you are now the good cop, so try and be nice."

"Yes yes yes, I am the good cop. Good cop, good cop, good cop," Beef repeated it over and over again like a mantra, so he wouldn't forget.

"Let's do this!" said Bone confidently.

"Is there time for a very quick pee?" asked Beef.

"No! I told you to go before we started!"

"But I didn't need to go then!"

"You'll just have to hold it in!"

"How?"

"Cross your legs or something! Whatever you do, don't think of a trickling stream!"

"Now all I can think about is a trickling stream!"

"Detective Beef! You are

making us both look highly unprofessional!"

"Sorry!"

"We are meant to be two of Scotland Yard's finest detectives."

"The finest!"

"Then let's do this!"

Beef and Bone strode back over to the table with a renewed sense of purpose.

"Right…," began Beef, "…would you like to come over for dinner?"

Jack and his grandfather looked at each other in disbelief. "That's too nice, *Kimberly*!" Bone shouted.

"But you told me to be the good cop!"

"That doesn't mean you are so nice you invite them over to dinner."

Beef thought for a moment. "Lunch?"

"NO!"

"A coffee morning?"

"NO! Look, *Kimberly*…"

"Don't call me *Kimberly*…"

"*Kimberly*, let me run this interrogation from now on. OK?"

Beef descended into a humongous sulk. This sulk was so humongous that now the detective refused to speak, nod, or even look anyone in the eye. Instead, he just shrugged at everything.

Bone returned his steely gaze to Grandpa, and soldiered on alone. "Three priceless antique aircraft were badly damaged today. Would you care to explain yourself?"

"He didn't mean any harm by it!" protested Jack. "It was just an accident! I promise!"

"You've been very quiet, old man, what do you have to say for yourself?" demanded Bone.

Jack's eyes darted to his grandfather. Was the old man about to say something that would drop himself even

deeper

in

doo-doo?

26

Turning the Tables

Down in the underground interview room of Scotland Yard, Jack looked nervously at his grandfather. What was the old man going to say? Grandpa straightened his RAF club tie before looking Detective Bone straight in the eye. "I have questions for you...!" he declared.

"What on earth are you doing?" Jack whispered.

"The only way to beat the Gestapo is to play them at their own game," Grandpa whispered back.

"No! *You* don't have questions for *us*, old man! That's not how this works," replied Bone, a note of disbelief in his voice.

Little did the detective know that Grandpa was not a man who would take no for an answer. "When is the launch date for Operation Sea Lion?" he demanded.

"Operation what?" asked Beef.

"Don't play the fool with me! You know darned well what I am talking about!"

shouted Grandpa, as he stood up and started pacing the room.

The two detectives shared a look with each other. Now they were even more confused than Grandpa. The pair had absolutely no idea what the old man was on about. "We really don't," replied Bone.

"You can never win this war of yours. And you can tell your friend Mr. Hitler that from me!"

"I've never even met him!" protested Beef.

"Neither of you are leaving this room until you tell me the start date for the ground offensive!"

Having been an officer in the RAF, Grandpa carried with him a natural sense of authority. The two detectives were cowering at having the tables turned on them. Jack was impressed.

"But I am meant to be playing badminton later…" pleaded Bone.

Grandpa stopped pacing the interrogation room and leaned over the table. He brought his face close to Beef's and Bone's. Despite his age, the old man was a formidable character. "You are not leaving this room until you tell me!"

"But I really need to pee!" begged Beef. "I'm gonna wet myself." The poor man looked as if he was going to burst into tears.

"TELL ME THE START DATE FOR OPERATION SEA LION!"

"What shall we do?" whispered Beef.

"Let's just say anything!" replied Bone.

They both answered Grandpa at exactly the same time.

"Monday!" "Thursday!"

This had the effect of making them look like liars. Which of course they were.

"Come on, Squadron Leader!" ordered Grandpa, and Jack stood up to attention. "Let's leave them in here to sweat it out. We'll be back in the morning!" Grandpa spun back toward the policemen. "You better tell us the truth then, or my goodness there will be trouble!"

With that, the old man marched over to the huge metal door of the interrogation room and Jack followed closely behind. The two detectives watched in stunned silence. Thinking quickly, Jack swiped the keys from the lock and pulled the door shut behind them. His heart was racing as he turned the key once more and locked the two men in.

CLICK.

Just at that moment the detectives realized they had been had. They raced toward the door to try and open it. They were too late. They started pounding on it for help.

"Brilliant work, sir. Now… let's run!" said Jack as he tugged his grandfather's sleeve.

"There is one last thing, Squadron Leader," replied Grandpa. He slid open the hatch in the door and shouted through it to the two detectives.

"By the way, Kimberly is definitely a girl's name!"

Then Jack and his grandfather raced off down the corridor, up the stairs, and out of Scotland Yard.

27

Behind Enemy Lines

From his RAF training, Grandpa knew very well how to evade capture behind enemy lines. Every pilot had to. The chances of being shot down over occupied territory were high.

Together he and Jack kept off the main roads and stayed out of the glare of streetlamps. When it was dark enough, the pair scaled a wall at the nearest London train station and climbed up on to the roof of the train they needed. Freezing cold and clinging on for dear life, they rode all the way back home.

"W-w-why do we n-n-need to be up here, W-w-wing C-c-commander?" asked Jack, shivering as he spoke.

"If I know the Gestapo they will have already boarded the train and be checking every passenger's identification papers, looking for us. We are much safer up here."

Just then, behind Grandpa, Jack saw that the train was speeding into a tunnel.

"G-g-get down!" shouted the boy.

The old man looked around and then flattened his body next to Jack's on the roof of the carriage. Just in time. When they had passed through the tunnel, Grandpa pushed himself up to his knees. "Thank you, Squadron Leader!" he said. "That was a very close shave."

At that moment, a low branch of a tree whacked him on the back of his head.

THWACK!

"Ow!"

"Are you all right, sir?"

"Yes, I am fine, old boy," replied Grandpa. "Darned enemy putting that blasted branch there!"

Jack was pretty sure Mr. Hitler and his Nazi friends had very little to do with it, but he let the comment pass.

It was close to midnight when they finally arrived at the station. Soon after, they reached Grandpa's road. The plan was to hide out in the old man's flat for a while. After all that had happened at the Imperial War Museum and Scotland Yard, the boy thought it best they didn't go to the family home.

To Jack's surprise, there was a light on in Raj's shop. The newsagent was still up, taking in the bundles of tomorrow's newspapers that had just been dropped off outside. The boy knew they could trust Raj. Just as well, as he and his grandfather were now on the run from the police.

"Raj!" called Jack.

The newsagent looked out into the darkness. "Who goes there?"

The pair tiptoed along the street. They stayed close to the wall, avoiding the light. It was a few moments before the newsagent could see them.

"Jack! Mr. Bumting! You gave me a very bad case of the **willies!**"

"Sorry, Raj, we didn't want to frighten you. We just didn't want to be seen, that's all," said the boy.

"Why?"

"It's a long story, Char Wallah!" replied Grandpa. "I look forward to telling you over a few pints of ale in the officers' mess."

"I am so pleased you were found safe and well, sir!" exclaimed the newsagent.

A car turned into the road. The headlamps shone on them.

"We better get inside…" said Jack.

"Yes, yes, of course," replied Raj. "Come in, come in. And bring a bundle of newspapers in for me, please!"

28

A Costly Call

The newsagent opened the door to his shop and ushered Jack and his grandfather inside. Once in his emporium, he gestured for the old man to sit on one of the piles of newspapers. "There we are, sir."

"Most kind, Char Wallah."

"Are you hungry? Thirsty? Please, Master Bumting, help yourself to anything in the shop."

"Really?" asked Jack. To a twelve-year-old boy this was quite an offer. "Anything?"

"Anything!" exclaimed Raj. "You two are my favorite customers in the world. Please, please, be my guests. Take whatever you want."

Jack smiled. "Thank you so much." After the day's adventure, he was in desperate need of some refreshment. So the boy helped himself to a few items for himself and Grandpa. A packet of crisps, a couple of chocolate bars, and two cartons of fruit juice.

To the boy's surprise, Raj began ringing all the items up on his till. "One pound, seventy-five pee, please."

Jack sighed and reached into his pocket for some change, which he placed on the counter.

"There you go, Raj."

"Mr. and Mrs. Bumting called round here some hours ago. Wondered if I had seen either of you. They both looked worried sick."

"Oh no." In all the excitement the boy had not really given his parents a second thought, and now he felt very guilty. "I better call them right away, Raj. Please, can I use your phone?"

"Of course!" said Raj, as he placed the telephone on the counter. "For you, there is no charge to make a call."

"Thank you," replied the boy.

"Just keep it very brief, please. No more than four or five seconds if you can."

"I'll try." Jack looked over at his grandfather, who was happily munching a chocolate bar and muttering between mouthfuls, "Jolly good show on the rations, Char Wallah."

"Sorry we are all out of biscuits," called the newsagent. "My aunt Dhriti broke in here last night and managed to get through four boxes of them. She even chewed the cardboard."

"Mum? It's me!" said Jack into the receiver.

"Where on earth have you been?" replied his mother. "Me and your father have been driving around all day and night looking for you!"

"Well, I can explain, I—" But before he could finish, his mother butted in.

"We had your teacher Miss Verity call the house to tell us what happened at the Imperial War Museum today. You broke a Spitfire!"

"That wasn't my fault. If the security guard hadn't been so heavy—"

Mum was in no mood to listen.

"I don't want to hear it! She said your grandfather had turned up at the museum, of all places! And that he had been arrested by the police! And when me and your dad got all the way to Scotland Yard they told us that the pair of you had escaped!"

"Well, yes and no. We just walked out of there really…"

"SHUT UP! NOW WHERE ARE YOU?"

Raj butted in. "Might you be so kind as to ask your mother to call back? We are already on one minute, thirty-eight seconds and it is going to be very expensive!"

"Mum? Raj says can you call back?"

"Oh, so you are at Raj's shop, are you?! STAY RIGHT THERE! WE'RE COMING OVER!" With that, the boy's mother slammed the telephone down.

CLICK!

WHIRR.

When Jack looked up, he realized Raj had been staring at his watch the whole time. "One minute and forty-six seconds. Tut-tut."

"My mum said they'll be straight over to pick us up."

"Splendid!" replied the newsagent. "Now, while you are waiting, can I interest you in a complimentary browse of my brand-new Christmas cards?"

"No, thank you, Raj—it's January."

"This one is particularly Christmassy," said the man as he showed Jack what was, in fact, a completely blank white card.

Jack looked at the card, and then at Raj. He thought for a moment that the newsagent might be losing his marbles. "But that's got absolutely nothing on it, Raj."

"No no no, that's where you are wrong, young Master Bumting. It is, in fact, a close-up picture of some snow. Absolutely perfect for the festive season. Just one pound for ten cards. Or I have a special offer on…"

"That's a surprise," muttered the boy.

"If you will take a thousand cards off my hands then I can do a very good price!"

"No, thank you, Raj," replied Jack politely.

But the newsagent loved to haggle. "Two thousand?"

Just then police sirens howled outside.

"The enemy" was closing in.

29

A Shadowy Figure

At first, the sirens sounded as if they were somewhere off in the distance, but they were fast becoming louder and louder. From the noise it sounded like an entire fleet of police cars was speeding toward Raj's shop. Jack's eyes darted toward the newsagent accusingly.

"I didn't call them! I promise," said Raj.

"Mum must have!" uttered the boy. With no time to lose, he grabbed his grandfather's arm and hurried him toward the door. "Wing Commander, we need to get out of here. NOW!"

But as they raced out into the dark, it was too late. They were surrounded.

Brakes screeched as a dozen or so police cars trapped Jack and Grandpa in a semicircle. There were blinding lights and a deafening noise.

"Put your hands up!" shouted

one of the policemen.

The pair did what they were told.

"It's straight to a prisoner-of-war camp for me. Colditz Castle, knowing my luck. Take care, old boy! See you back in Blighty!" whispered Grandpa.

Raj followed them out. He had attached his white handkerchief to a Curly Wurly and waved it like a flag to surrender. "Please don't shoot! I have just had the front of my shop redecorated."

Jack's parents must have been traveling in one of the police cars because now they broke through the line of officers.

The pair ran toward their son and embraced him.

"We were so worried about you!" said Dad.

"I am sorry," said Jack. "I didn't mean to worry you."

"Well, we were worried, Jack!" replied Mum, softening at the sight of her son.

"What's going to happen to Grandpa?" asked the boy. "They can't send him to prison."

"No," replied Mum. "None of us want that. Not even the police. I called that nice Mr. Vicar tonight. Grandpa's very lucky. By some miracle he has secured a place for him at that old folk's home, Twilight Towers."

Right on cue, a shadowy figure stepped out of one of the police cars. With the bright glare of the headlights behind her, at first all Jack could make out was her silhouette. She was a short, stocky lady, with what looked like a nurse's hat on her head and a cape draped over her shoulders.

"Who are you?" demanded Jack.

At a slow pace the figure walked toward him. Her high-heeled boots echoed on the cold, wet pavement. When she finally reached him, her face contorted into a pantomime of a smile. Her eyes were small and mean, and her nose upturned, as if she was sticking it against a window.

"Ah! You must be young Jack!" she said brightly. Her voice was light, but Jack could tell there was darkness lurking in her words. "I had a call from the charming Reverend Hogg. The vicar and I are so close. We share a concern for the elderly of this town."

"I said, 'Who are you?'" repeated the boy.

"My name is Miss Swine, I am the matron of Twilight Towers. And I've come to take your grandfather away," purred the lady.

PART II

A MATTER OF LIFE AND DEATH

30

Twilight Towers

That night, Grandpa was taken away to Twilight Towers. It was a condition of the police dropping their charges against the old man that he be sent there.

Needless to say, Jack had a sleepless night. All he could think about was his grandpa. So as soon as school had finished the next day, Jack raced over to Twilight Towers on his trike. The boy pedaled as fast as he could, desperate to see his grandfather, and desperate that none of the children from school see him on his toddler's trike. Jack was saving up for a chopper, which looked more like a motorcycle than a bicycle, but so far only had enough for one of the pedals.

Twilight Towers was some distance from the center of town. As the rows of little houses ended, so the moors began. Atop a hill sat an old building. Surrounded by a high wall, and with tall gates at the front, it looked more like a prison than an old people's home. Disneyland it was not.

Jack trundled along the dirt track on his trike. He stopped as he reached the gates. These were made of thick metal, with spikes on top. Two ornate metal *T*'s for Twilight Towers had been welded on to them. There was a sign outside that read:

Twilight Towers
Caring for your
unwanted old folk

The place had only opened recently. The town's previous old folk's home—Sunshine Place—had been demolished by the unexplained runaway bulldozer accident. Twilight Towers was in fact a converted Victorian lunatic asylum. It was a tall brick building, dotted with tiny windows. All the windows had bars on them. It may have been called an old folk's "home," but in truth this building had such a sense of foreboding that it could never be a home to anyone. The building had four floors, and a tall bell tower stood on the roof.

Two more recently built observation towers stood at either end of the grounds. On top of both were huge searchlights, manned by big, burly nurses. Whether all this security was to keep people in or out remained to be seen.

Jack reached out to rattle the gates to see if they were unlocked.

ZAP!

The boy felt a bolt of electricity flash through his body.

"*Argh!*" It was as if he was turned upside down, inside out, back to front all at once. As fast as he could, he took his hands off the gates, and breathed deeply. The pain had been so intense, the boy felt like he was going to be sick.

"WHO GOES THERE?" came a deep voice through a megaphone. Blinking back tears of pain, Jack looked up to see a nurse calling down from her observation tower.

"Jack."

"JACK WHO?" The loud-hailer made the nurse's voice sound mechanical like a robot.

"Jack Bunting. I have come to visit my grandfather."

"Visiting is on Sundays only. Come back then."

"But I have cycled all this way…" Jack couldn't believe he was being refused entry. All he wanted to do was see Grandpa for a short while.

"Any visitors wanting to come to Twilight Towers on any other day must have permission from the matron."

199

"I have!" lied the boy. "Yes, I saw Miss Swine last night and she told me to pop round this afternoon."

"COME THROUGH THE GATES AND REPORT TO RECEPTION."

BUZZ!
CLINK.

The gates opened automatically and the boy slowly pedaled inside.

The gravel path was difficult to ride on, especially on a trike made for a toddler.

Eventually Jack made it to the huge wooden door. As the boy rang the bell he realized his hands were shaking.

CLICK CLACK CLICK CLICK.

There must have been ten different locks on the door it took so long to open it.

CLACK CLICK CLICK CLICK CLACK CLICK CLICK.

Finally a big, burly nurse opened the door. She had thick hairy legs, a gold tooth, and a tattoo of a skull on her arm. Despite this she sported a name badge that read "Nurse Daisy."

"**WOT?**" said the lady in a deep voice. There was not a person on the earth less suited to the name Daisy.

"Oh, hello!" said Jack politely. "I wonder if you can help me."

"**WOT DO YOU WANT?**" demanded Nurse Daisy.

"I am here to visit my grandfather, Arthur Bunting. He arrived last night."

"**WE'RE CLOSED TO VISITORS TODAY!**"

"I know, I know, but I met the lovely Miss Swine of this place last night, and I just wondered if I could have a quick word with her?"

"WAIT THERE!" said the nurse, as she slammed the heavy oak door on him. **"MATRON!"** he heard her shout.

There now followed such a long wait that the boy all but gave up hope of anyone coming back. Eventually, he heard heavy footsteps echo along the corridor, and the door swung open to a **TRULY TERRIFYING SIGHT.**

31

The World's Ugliest Nurses

The matron of Twilight Towers stood in the doorway. The short lady was wearing her nurse's cap, and was flanked by two incredibly bulky nurses who dwarfed her. One nurse had a black eye, and "LOVE" and "HATE" tattooed on her knuckles. The other had a tattoo of a spider's web on her neck and what looked like stubble on her chin. Both scowled at the boy. They were the ugliest nurses you could ever hope to meet. Jack's eyes darted to their name badges — "Nurse Rose" and "Nurse Blossom."

Miss Swine was twirling what at first glance looked like a baton. Holding it in one hand, she then rhythmically tapped the palm of her other. The effect was one of quiet menace. At one end of the baton were two little metal prongs, and at the other a button. What was this strange contraption?

"Well, well, well…we meet again. Good afternoon, young Jack," purred Miss Swine.

"Good afternoon, matron. It's lovely to see you again," he lied. "Nice to meet you too, ladies," he lied again.

"Now, we are very busy here looking after all the old folk at Twilight Towers. What is it you want?"

"I want to see my grandfather," replied the boy.

The two nurses chuckled to themselves at the thought. Jack had no idea how what he had just said could be considered funny.

"I am so, so sorry, but it's not possible right now," replied Miss Swine.

"W-w-why?" the boy asked nervously.

"Your grandfather is having a little snooze. My old folk here do love a good snooze. You wouldn't want to interrupt that now, would you? That would be rather selfish of you, don't you think?"

"Well, I am sure if Grandpa knew I was here he would want to see me. I am his only grandchild."

"Strange. He hasn't mentioned you once since he got here. Perhaps he has forgotten all about you."

If this was designed to wound the boy, it succeeded.

"Please!" Jack was pleading now. "I just want to see my grandfather. I need to know he is all right."

"For the last time, your grandfather is snoozing!" Matron was losing her patience. "He's just had his pills."

"His pills? What do you mean 'his pills'?" Jack wasn't aware that his grandfather needed any pills. In fact, the old man had always refused to take medicine of any kind, saying he was "fit as a fiddle."

"I personally prescribed some pills to help him sleep."

"But it's still early. He doesn't need to go to sleep now. It's not his bedtime. Let me see him!" The boy lunged forward to try and get inside. Immediately he was repelled backward by Nurse Rose. Her big hairy hand caught his face, and threw it back like it was a ball. The boy stumbled on to the gravel and landed on his bottom. The nurses had a good laugh at this.

"HA! HA! HA! HA! HA!
HA! HA! HA! HA! HA!
HA! HA! HA! HA! HA!
HA! HA! HA! HA! HA!
HA! HA! HA! HA! HA!
HA! HA! HA! HA! HA!
HA! HA! HA! HA! HA!
HA! HA! HA! HA! HA!"

Jack scrambled to his feet. "You can't get away with this. I demand to see my grandfather this instant!"

"The well-being of my old folk is of paramount importance to all of us here at Twilight Towers," announced Miss Swine. Her two little eyes glinted in the low winter sun. "So we keep them on a strict timetable. And as you can see, the visiting hour is listed right there…" She pointed to a sign on the wall with her baton.

It read:

Twilight Towers
OPENING HOUR:
SUNDAY AFTERNOON
3:00 P.M. TO 3:15 P.M.
LATECOMERS NOT ADMITTED.
ALL OTHER TIMES WE ARE
STRICTLY CLOSED TO ALL VISITORS.

"That's not even an hour!" protested the boy.

"Boo hoo hoo," replied Miss Swine, before offering a sinister smile. "Now, if you don't mind, I have my old folk to think of. I can't have a nasty, selfish little child ruin everything for them now, can I? Nurses?"

"Yes, Matron," they replied in unison.

"Please escort this young man off the premises."

"Yes, Matron." With that, the two burly nurses stepped forward. Together Nurse Rose and Nurse Blossom picked Jack up by his arms. Without breaking a sweat, they carried him down the gravel path toward the front gates. Jack tried to kick his legs, but the nurses were so big and strong that there was no way he could take them on.

The matron watched as the boy was carried off. She smiled to herself and gave Jack a little wave as she called after him,

"Missing you already! Do come back and see us again soon!"

32

Weeping Willow

Nurse Rose and Nurse Blossom dumped the boy right outside the gates, like he was a bag of rubbish. Jack's trike was tossed after him and it landed with a clatter on the ground.

CLANK!

Then the huge metal gates whirred shut.

CLUNK!

From inside, the two nurses watched as the boy picked himself up, got on his trike, and pedaled off down the road.

By this time, the sky was shot with red as the sun set. Night was about to fall. As Twilight Towers was set on the edge of the moors, streetlamps were few and far between. Soon it was dark. Real country dark.

After pedaling for quite a while, Jack looked over his shoulder. Twilight Towers was now a long way off, and just as he could no longer see the nurses, they could no longer see him.

Jack was a boy who was not going to take no for an answer when it came to seeing his grandfather. What's more, it was clear Miss Swine and her gang of nurses were not to be trusted. As he reached an area of woodland, he jumped off his trike before hiding it under a bush and covering it with branches—just as Grandpa had told him the RAF would hide Spitfires on the ground from enemy aircraft above.

Slowly Jack made his way on foot back to the sinister old folk's home. He avoided the road, and instead made his way across the moors that led to Twilight Towers. With only the moon illuminating his path, finally Jack reached the perimeter wall. It was a great deal taller than he was, and barbed wire snaked its way across the top. Climbing it was going to be impossible, so Jack had to think. And fast.

There was a weeping willow tree growing next to the wall, two of its branches just draping over into the grounds of Twilight Towers. There was one problem: the willow tree was in full view of both observation towers. From the top of these, huge searchlights swept up and down the grounds. This was going to be dangerous. Jack was frightened. He'd never even dared to do anything like this before.

Slowly but surely, Jack began to climb the willow tree. That it was winter and the branches were bare of leaves made it easier. After he had shimmied up the trunk, he edged his way along a branch. But disaster struck as it buckled under his weight and disturbed a flock of ravens that had been perched there.

SQuaWK SQuaWK SQuaWK

The black birds made an awful racket as they took to the air in fright.

The beam of the searchlights circled in the darkness before stopping on the tree.

As fast as he could, Jack edged his body around to the far side of the trunk to avoid detection. He pressed himself up against it, and stayed as still as a statue.

The lights froze on the willow tree for some time, before eventually moving off. But the nurses atop the observation towers would be suspicious now. One false move from the boy and he would be caught. Who knew what Miss Swine would do to him then?

After counting to ten in his head, Jack edged himself back around to the other side of the tree. On his hands and knees now, the boy crawled along the branch that hung over the vast grounds of the nursing home. But not being used to climbing trees, Jack made a miscalculation. He had spent too long painting model planes in his bedroom and was not one for the great outdoors. So Jack crawled right to the end of the branch, thinking he could let his weight act as a lever.

CREAK...

But the branch was not strong enough to hold him.

CREEEEAAK.

And it snapped.

SNAP!

33

Slither Like a Snake

The boy fell into tall grass. Searchlights from the observation towers circled the grounds of Twilight Towers. Jack lay there still and silent for some time, despite being badly winded by the fall. Out of the corner of his eye, he could see the lights circling closer to him. A part of the boy was in a terrible panic and wanted to flee, but he remembered what his grandfather had taught him to do in a situation like this. Do not move a muscle. When the searchlights eventually shifted off, the boy looked up slowly. There was still a long stretch of exposed ground between him and the building. How could he possibly get there without being seen?

Another lesson Grandpa had taught Jack was, when in open ground, to slither like a snake. Jack never dreamed he would one day have to use these

skills in a real-life adventure. But that's exactly what the boy did now, as he made his way across the cold wet grass.

It was hard going, but finally the boy reached the main building.

The problem now was that Jack had absolutely no idea where Grandpa would be. Staying close to the wall, he traced around the building, ducking under windows as he went. There was only one way in or out of Twilight Towers. That was the front door, which the nurses kept locked, double-locked, and triple-locked. Jack spotted a doorway at the rear of the building, but it had been bricked up.

Being careful not to be seen, the boy peered through one of the windows. He saw a dormitory that must have had about twenty beds in it. The beds were arranged neatly in two long rows, and despite it being no later than six o'clock, all the old ladies in there were already tucked up in bed. Glancing along at their faces one by one, Jack noticed they were all fast asleep. There was not a man among them, so the boy quickly moved on.

A couple of windows along, Jack spied into a room that looked like a chemist's store. From floor to ceiling, the room was full of bottles of pills, medicine, and syringes. A hefty-looking nurse in a lab coat paced up and down. There must have been thousands upon thousands of pills in that store—enough to put a herd of elephants to sleep, let alone a hundred or so elderly people.

After peeping through a couple more of the windows on the ground floor and finding only a filthy kitchen and an empty living room, the boy decided to search the next floor up. So he gathered his strength, and pulled himself up a drainpipe at the side of the building.

Edging his way along a narrow ledge one floor up, he arrived at the first window. Through it Jack spied an imposing oak-paneled office. Matron was reclining at her desk in a luxurious leather armchair, puffing on a big fat cigar. Her little feet were resting up on the desk, and she was blowing plumes of thick gray smoke into the air above her. This private version of herself was a very different Miss Swine to the one she showed others.

A large portrait of the matron hung over the fire in a thick gold frame. Staying as close as he could to the wall, Jack tilted his head slightly to afford a better view. On her wide, leather-topped desk was a large pile of paperwork she was sorting through. Resting her cigar in a crystal-glass ashtray, Miss Swine went to work.

First, Matron picked up a piece of paper from the pile, before placing a piece of tracing paper over it.

 Second, she slowly but surely copied the handwriting underneath with a pencil.

 Third, she turned the tracing paper over and rubbed the tip of her pencil all over it.

 Fourth, she took out a new blank piece of white paper from her drawer, and placed the tracing paper over and on to it.

 Fifth, Matron went over the outline of the handwriting with her pencil, hard, which made it appear on the blank piece of paper below.

Last, she placed the piece of paper in her typewriter and began pressing the keys.

After she had hammered away at the typewriter for a while, Miss Swine studied her work with satisfaction. Next, she screwed up the original piece of paper into a ball, and tossed it in the fire. Watching it burn she laughed to herself, and wrapped her lips around her long, fat cigar once more.

What on earth was Miss Swine up to?

Standing on the narrow ledge, staring in bafflement, the boy's foot slipped and he scrambled to keep himself from falling.

All of a sudden Matron looked up, as if she had heard something outside. Jack edged out of view and flattened his body against the wall. The lady rose from her leather chair and paced over to the window. She pressed her upturned nose up against the glass, which made it look even more upturned than it already was, and peered out into the dark…

34

Hidden in a Mustache

Jack stayed perfectly still and didn't dare breathe. As Matron stood staring out of the window of her office high up in Twilight Towers, she was so close the boy could smell the cigar smoke. He had always loathed the smell of cigars, and a tickly cough started itching his throat. *Don't cough!* he prayed. *Please, please, please, don't cough!*

After listening to the silence for a while, Matron shook her head dismissively. Finally she closed the heavy black-velvet curtains that hung in her window so not a soul could see in.

Jack's first impulse was to run home and tell his parents that he thought the matron was up to no good. But the boy hesitated; he had lied and told them he was going to be at an after-school chess club. What's more, the chances of his mum or dad believing him were slim. They had managed to convince themselves that ᴛᴡɪʟɪɢʜᴛ ᴛᴏᴡᴇʀꜱ was the best place for Grandpa.

Instead, the boy inched his way along the narrow ledge to another window. The lights were out in that room, but through the gloom Jack could make out a chilling sight. Rows upon rows of coffins!

Continuing along the ledge, Jack peered in at the next room. The light was on and at first glance it looked like an antiques shop. The room was filled from floor to ceiling with old paintings, vases and clocks. All the items looked valuable, and a couple of the nurses were dragging in an expensive-looking, gold-framed antique mirror and leaning it up against the wall. Where was all this stuff from?

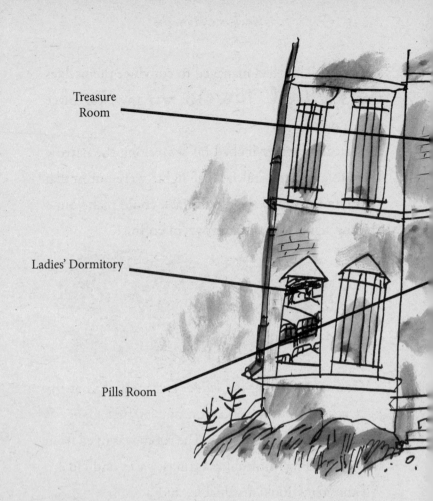

Treasure Room

Ladies' Dormitory

Pills Room

The bright beam of a searchlight skimmed the building. It shone dangerously close to Jack. As quickly as he could, the boy edged his way around the corner of the building out of sight.

Climbing up the icy drainpipe to the next floor,

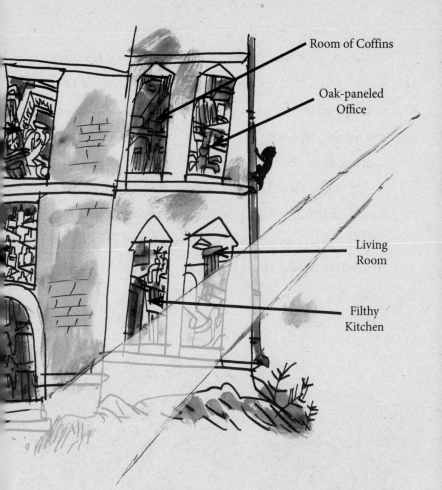

Room of Coffins

Oak-paneled Office

Living Room

Filthy Kitchen

Jack's fingers were beginning to claw with the cold. Still, he bravely carried on, and peered into the nearest window. This room was another dormitory, even bigger than the first. Crammed in together, lying in beds too small for them, were rows and rows of old men. Just like in the ladies' dormitory the men were frozen still, in deep, deep sleep. The boy's eyes scanned all the faces, desperate to spot his grandfather. He needed to know that the old man, whom he loved more than anyone else in the world, was alive and well.

Up and down the rows of beds he looked, until he found that unmistakeable RAF mustache. Grandpa! The old man's eyes were tightly shut, and just like all the others he appeared to be in a deep, deep sleep.

To keep his balance, Jack held on to the metal bars in front of the window with one hand. Putting his other hand through the bars, he traced the edges of the window with his fingertips to see if he could prize it open from the outside.

Unsurprisingly, like every other window or door in this fortress, it was locked.

Jack had come so far, he couldn't leave now without at least trying to make contact with his grandfather. Unsure of what else he could do, the boy began tapping on the window.

TAP TAP TAP.

Quietly at first, and then louder and louder.

TAP TAP TAP.

All of a sudden, one of Grandpa's tightly shut eyes opened. Then the other. Jack banged on the window even harder now, and the old man sat up in bed bolt upright. He was wearing a frayed pair of pajamas that looked second or third or even fourth hand. Seeing his grandson outside the window, the old man couldn't help but smile. After a quick look left and right to check the coast was clear, Grandpa tiptoed over from his bed to the window.

From the inside, the old man managed to open it a tiny bit so they could hear each other.

"Squadron Leader!" whispered Grandpa, greeting his grandson with his customary salute.

"Wing Commander!" said the boy, as he hung on to the window bars with one hand and saluted with the other.

"As you can see the enemy has locked me up here in Colditz Castle—the most heavily fortified prisoner-of-war camp there is!"

Jack didn't contradict his grandfather. It would only confuse the old man to break the illusion. Though, truth be told, *Twilight Towers* was a lot more like a prisoner-of-war camp than an old folk's home.

"I am so sorry, sir."

"Not your fault, Bunting. This happens in war. There must be some way out, but I darned well haven't found it yet."

Looking behind his grandfather at all the old men who were completely zonked out, Jack asked, "How come you are wide-awake and everyone else is fast asleep?"

"Ha-ha!" Grandpa laughed mischievously. "The guards force us all to take these pills. They dole them out like sweets. One's enough to knock a man out cold."

"How come you didn't swallow yours, sir?"

"The guards stand over you to make sure you take them. I put mine in my mouth, and pretended to swallow. When they moved on to the next prisoner, I spat them out and hid them deep in my mustache."

With that, he plucked two small brightly colored pills out from under his thick hairy curls.

The old man was ingenious!

Once a hero, always a hero, thought Jack.

"You're quite brilliant, Wing Commander," said the boy.

"Thank you, Squadron Leader. I am so pleased you are here. Now we can put my plan into action, the tooter the sweeter."

Jack was puzzled. "What plan, Wing Commander?"

His grandpa looked at him and grinned.

"The escape plan, of course!"

35

Still More Socks

As part of his plan, the old man gave his grandson a shopping list of items he needed smuggled into 𝒯wilight 𝒯owers from the outside. Reading it in bed that night, Jack didn't have a clue how Grandpa planned to use them in his escape.

The list was as follows:

- Smarties
- String
- Socks
- Elastic bands
- Empty tin cans
- Map
- More socks
- Matches
- Spoon
- Tea tray
- Candles
- Roller skates
- Still more socks

The Smarties were easy. The next morning, Jack paid a visit to Raj's shop on the way to school to find there was a plentiful supply. What's more, Jack was in luck—the newsagent even had the multicolored chocolates on special offer. Thirty-eight tubes for the price of thirty-seven.

Empty tin cans Jack fished out of the garbage can at home, then rinsed under the tap.

Some cheap old roller skates were found in the local charity shop.

Elastic bands, string, a spoon, candles, and matches were all dotted around the house in various drawers and cupboards.

As were the socks. Dad had plenty of odd ones lying around, and Jack was sure his father wouldn't miss them.

No one knows where socks disappear to. It is one of the universe's greatest mysteries. Either they are sucked into a black hole where time and space have become flattened, or they get caught in the back of the washing machine. Either way, Jack's father had plenty of them.

The tea tray was the hardest item to smuggle out of the kitchen, due to its size. Jack had to wedge it into the back of his trousers, before putting his jumper on over the top. It looked fine when he was standing still, but as soon as he tried to walk, it was as if he were a robot.

After Jack had spent every moment he could that day collecting all of Grandpa's items, he sat on his top bunk, waiting for the sky to turn black. As his unsuspecting parents thought he was fast asleep, he followed his grandfather's lead and fled out of his bedroom window.

The moon was low that night. The shadows of the trees stretched out across the grounds of Twilight Towers. Jack had to be extra careful not to be seen, as he climbed the weeping willow and jumped down from another of its overhanging branches. He crawled across the grass before shimmying up the drainpipe to the men's dormitory.

As soon as Jack arrived at the window his grandpa announced triumphantly, "I am going to dig my way out!"

Just as the night before, Jack was balancing precariously on a narrow ledge high up on the side of the building. Because of the bars on the outside, the window only opened a tiny bit. As they spoke, Jack passed all the items on Grandpa's list through the narrow gap.

"Dig?" The boy was not convinced this was a good idea. "With what?"

"With the spoon, of course, Squadron Leader!"

36

With a Spoon?!

"You are going to dig your way out with a spoon?!" asked Jack. The boy couldn't believe his ears. "You want to dig a tunnel all the way past the wall there with a spoon?!"

"Yes, Bunting!" replied Grandpa from the other side of the window bars. "I will start tonight. I have to get Up, *up, and away* in my Spitfire quick smart. As soon as you go, I will steal myself down to the cellar and begin scraping away at the stone floor."

Jack didn't want to burst his grandfather's bubble, but it was clear that the old man's plan was doomed to failure. It would take years just to dig through the cellar floor. Especially using only a spoon. It wasn't even a particularly big spoon.

"Did you remember the tins?" continued the old man.

Jack reached into his coat pocket and passed two old baked-bean cans through the gap.

"Of course, sir. What are you going to use them for?" asked the boy.

"**Buckets, Bunting! Buckets!** Fill them with all the earth I will dig out with the spoon, and then pass them out of the tunnel on a pulley system."

"So that's what the string is for!"

"That's right, Squadron Leader. Do keep up!"

"But what are you going to do with all the soil?"

"This is the devilishly clever bit, old boy. That's what the socks are for!"

"The socks? I don't follow you, sir," said the boy as he reached into a pocket and pulled out a jumble of his dad's old socks.

"This sock's got a hole in it!" complained Grandpa as he stopped to examine one.

"Sorry, sir, I didn't know what you needed them for."

"I'll tell you, Squadron Leader. Once dawn breaks and I have done my digging for the night," continued Grandpa, "I will pack all the soil into the socks. Then I will tie an elastic band to the top of each sock. I will conceal the sock of soil or 'soil sock' as they will henceforth be known, down my trousers. Then I will make a request to the Kommandant that I be put on gardening duty."

"The Kommandant?" The boy was baffled.

"Yes, keep up! Runs this POW camp."

The matron! thought Jack. "Of course, sir."

"Once at the flower beds, I will make sure the guards aren't looking, I will pull on the bands of the soil socks and tallyho! The soil is released! Then I will shuffle about like a penguin treading it into the ground."

To illustrate this particular part of the escape plan, Grandpa did a little penguin walk around his dormitory.

"That still doesn't explain the tea tray and roller skates, sir," said Jack.

"Getting there, Bunting! I will attach the roller skates to the bottom of the tea tray, and use it to travel backward and forward along the tunnel on my back."

"Well, sir, you have certainly thought of everything."

"It's genius, Bunting. GENIUS!" proclaimed Grandpa a little too loudly.

"You must be careful not to wake them all, sir," whispered the boy, indicating the rows of sleeping old men in the dormitory.

"A bomb couldn't wake this lot up, old boy. Those sleeping pills the guards give us could knock out a rhinoceros. My fellow prisoners of war are only awake for less than an hour each day. Quick bowl of watery soup, then straight back to bed!"

"So this is where all the Smarties come in!" guessed the boy.

"Correct, Squadron Leader! There are only so many of those darned pills that I can conceal in my mustache.

The Kommandant has become suspicious too."

"Really, sir?"

"Yes, wants to know why I am so much more awake than everyone else. So the guards have doubled my dose and watch me like hawks when I am given them. So I plan to break into the pharmacy they have here, and exchange my pills for sweets. Cut them off at the supply! Then there is no problem with me swallowing them. In fact, I am rather partial to the odd Smartie."

Jack had to hand it to his grandfather. This was a brilliant and daring plan. But from the narrow ledge where he was standing, the boy looked out across the grounds of Twilight Towers. The perimeter wall was at least a hundred meters away. It was going to take the old man a lifetime to dig all that way, especially armed with nothing more than a spoon, some old socks, and a tea tray with a pair of roller skates attached to the bottom of it.

And Grandpa didn't have a lifetime left.

Jack was going to have to help him.

But he had no idea how.

37

Something Dark, Something Creepy

It was a Sunday, the day on which Matron permitted the visiting hour to Twilight Towers. Which wasn't even an hour. It was fifteen minutes—3:00 p.m. to 3:15 p.m. And as Jack had found out, if you tried to see your family member at any other time, the nurses would escort you off the premises.

The family sat in silence in the car for most of the journey there.

In the driving seat, Jack's father stared straight ahead not saying a word. From the backseat, the boy glimpsed Dad's eyes in the rearview mirror. They were misted with tears.

In the passenger seat, Jack's mother kept on blabbing away to fill the silence. She used second-hand phrases, phrases people use when they try to convince themselves of something they know is not true. Phrases like, "It's for the best," and "I imagine he's so much happier than he was at home," and even "In time, I am sure he will learn to love it there."

The boy had to bite his tongue. His parents had no idea he had made two secret visits to Twilight Towers already. But although he didn't think they would believe his suspicions about this terrible place, Jack hoped that when they actually visited Twilight Towers they might begin to see things his way.

When the car lurched up to the metal gates, Dad stepped out to open them. Suddenly having a flashback to the electric shock he'd received before, Jack blurted out, "Just ring the bell!" His father looked puzzled, but did what the boy said. Slowly the gates whirred open. With Dad back in the car, they drove inside.

The worn tires slipped on the gravel. As the car reeled to one side, Twilight Towers loomed into view.

"Well, it looks very, er, nice," said Mum.

As soon as the car had stopped outside the front

door, Dad turned off the engine. Jack's ears pricked up. He could hear music coming from the home. Immediately he recognized the tune.

DA-DA DA-DA DA-DA DAA♫

It was "The Birdie Song," a song so annoying once inside your head it would never leave.

DA-DA DA-DA DA-DA DAA♫

The instrumental record had recently been a huge number one hit.

DA-DA DA-DA♫

The song had been played over and over again at every wedding, party, and children's birthday up and down the country.

DA-DA DA-DA♫

"The Birdie Song" screamed *FUN FUN FUN!*

DA-DA-DA DAA, DA-DAAA, DA-DAA DAA♫

But it wasn't fun. It was torture.

DA-DA-DA DAA, DA-DA-DA DAA!♫

To Jack's surprise, Matron bounded out of the front door, sporting a paper party hat.

"Welcome welcome welcome!" she said in a jolly

tone that sat as awkwardly with her as the ridiculous hat did on her head.

Miss Swine's eyes swiveled over to the boy. Without his parents noticing she glared at him. The intent was clear. Make any trouble and there would be **TROUBLE**.

"Come in come in!" Matron ushered the family through the front door. The first thing Jack spotted with his eagle eyes was a notice on the wall, half hidden behind some party decorations. It read:

RULES OF Twilight Towers

By order of Matron Swine

- All PERSONAL ITEMS such as jewelry, watches, valuables, etc. to be handed in to the matron's office upon arrival.

- The nurses are all highly trained professionals and must be OBEYED at all times.

- SILENCE! Do not speak unless spoken to by a member of staff.

- Do NOT complain about the tea. We know it tastes like someone's bathwater that has been PEED in. That's because it is.

- Lights out at 5:00 p.m. SHARP. Anyone caught still up after this late hour will be put on toilet-cleaning duty armed with only a toothbrush.

- BATH TIME is the first Monday of the month. The bath water is to be shared by all residents.

- Radiators to be kept switched OFF at all times. If you are cold, JUMP up and down for a bit.

- Any cakes, biscuits, chocolates, etc. brought in by visitors are to be handed over to a nurse IMMEDIATELY.

- One piece of TOILET PAPER only to be used on each visit to the lavatory. This is for number twos as well as number ones.

- You MUST take your pills. If you fail to take your pills, every single person in your dormitory will be PUNISHED for all ETERNITY.

- WHISTLING or HUMMING is absolutely FORBIDDEN.

- ONE BEDPAN per dorm—please do NOT ask for more.

- All MEALS you are given, however RANCID, must be eaten. Any SCRAPS left over will be served up to you at the next mealtime.

- You are NOT to look Matron in the eye, or talk to her directly.

- Pajamas and nightdresses to be worn DAY AND NIGHT.

- You are NOT to leave the premises at any time. Anyone who does try to leave will be CHAINED to their bed.

- If you have a COMPLAINT, please write it down and put it in the complaint box. The box is emptied every Friday afternoon and the contents burned.

HAVE A LOVELY STAY.

Mum didn't see the sign, she just saw the balloons and colored streamers that half obscured it. This prompted Mum to ask, "Oh! Are you having a party today, Matron?"

"Well, yes and no, Mrs. Bunting. It's party time all the time at Twilight Towers!" lied Miss Swine. "Please come through to the living room and join in all the f-f-fun."

Jack noticed that "fun" was not a word Miss Swine found easy to say. In fact, she spat it out as if it were poison. It was a shame that neither Mum nor Dad seemed to see what an evil character this lady was.

"The Birdie Song" was thankfully just finishing. But the moment it did, a burly nurse lifted the needle on the record player and played it again straightaway. *DA-DA DA-DA DA-DA DAA*♫

The living room was crowded with old folk and even more nurses.

At first sight, the elderly people appeared to be happily moving along to the music.

"Isn't it wonderful, Barry?" said Mum. "All these oldies are having an absolute ball!"

Dad nodded his head slightly. But the man wasn't

really listening. Instead, his eyes were scanning the room for his father.

"Well, Mrs. Bunting…," began Miss Swine.

"Call me Barbara, or Babs for short," replied Mum.

"Well, Babs," Matron began again, "I hate to blow my own trumpet, but everyone agrees that what makes **Twilight Towers** so special is how happy all my old folk are. And I put that down to the fun atmosphere we have here! We sure know how to **PARTY!**"

Jack loathed the way this evil woman was weaseling her way into his mother's confidence.

"Oh, one teeny-weeny thing," said Matron abruptly. "Mr. Bunting?"

"Yes?"

"Did you bring your father's will, like I asked?"

"Oh, yes, Miss Swine, I have it right here." Dad reached into his inside jacket pocket and passed her an envelope.

DING!

So that's what Matron was up to in her office, thought Jack suddenly.

Now he knew exactly what the evil woman was doing with the tracing paper. She was rewriting the old folks' wills and forging their signatures at the bottom. Doubtless so that she would become the sole heir to their fortunes. That explained the mysterious room full of treasures too.

This was fraud on a grand scale.

"Thank you! I just need to keep it here in my office for safekeeping."

"Mum! Dad!" cried Jack. He had to tell them.

"Please be quiet for a moment, son, the nice matron is talking!" Mum insisted.

"Yes, you please keep it safe for us, Matron," Dad went on. "Thank you so much."

Looking around the room in desperation, suddenly the boy realized something else.

SOMETHING DARK.

SOMETHING CREEPY.

SOMETHING SO SINISTER IT CHILLED HIM TO THE BONE.

38

Dummies

Jack realized that none of the old folk in the living room were moving of their own accord.

The brawny nurses of Twilight Towers were actually manipulating them, as a ventriloquist might a dummy. One old man with a hearing aid that whistled loudly seemed to be clapping along to the music. But when you looked again, you realized Nurse Rose was holding his hands in hers.

An old lady appeared to be bopping her head along. Look again and it was being moved in time by Nurse Blossom.

A third elderly inmate with a ruddy nose and a monocle gave the impression he was a champion ballroom dancer. The short man was whisking a tall nurse around the living room as if it were a dance floor. Or was he? On closer inspection, it was the nurse,

Nurse Violet, who was leading. She was holding up the little old man. His slippers scraped the ground, his eyes were closed, and he was snoring loudly.

As well as the Bunting family, there were quite a few other visitors to Twilight Towers that afternoon. This was the only fifteen minutes of the week that anyone could come, after all. Among them, an old man wearing milk-bottle-thick glasses who

looked like he was visiting his wife. The woman was tiny, like a little bird. The pair were playing draughts together, though in reality one of the beefiest nurses, Nurse Tulip, had stuck her arms through the old lady's cardigan sleeves and was moving the pieces on her behalf. The giveaway to Jack was that the little old lady now had these massive hairy hands.

Meanwhile, a couple of toddlers sat with a rather round old lady who must have been their grandmother. The children's mother looked completely disinterested, and sat there flicking through a dog-eared magazine. The old lady appeared to be patting the children's heads, but Jack spotted a piece of fishing wire attached to her hands. His eyes followed the fishing wire, which glinted a little in the light. It stretched across the room, ending behind a curtain. Hiding there was another nurse, Nurse Hyacinth, with a fishing rod. As the nurse twitched the rod up and down, so moved the old lady's hand.

This is wicked, thought Jack. No doubt Miss Swine put on this absurd show every Sunday afternoon at Twilight Towers just for the visitors.

It might have fooled most people, but not Jack.

"Miss Swine, where is my grandpa?" the boy demanded. "What have you done to him?"

Matron simply smiled at the boy. "As soon as you arrived, I sent for your grandfather. I believe he will be joining us here at the party any second now…"

Right on cue the door to the living room swung

open. Grandpa was in an ancient wooden wheelchair, being pushed by Nurse Daisy, she of the gold tooth and the tattoo of a skull on her arm. The old man appeared to be fast asleep.

Oh no, thought the boy. *They must have force-fed him the sleeping pills after all.* As Nurse Daisy pushed Grandpa into position in front of the flickering television, Jack rushed over to him. Knowing of their special bond, Mum and Dad held back for a moment.

The boy grasped the old man's hand tight.

"What have they done to you?" he asked aloud, not expecting a response.

Suddenly Grandpa opened one of his eyes. It revolved around, to focus on his grandson.

"Ah, there you are, Squadron Leader!" whispered the old man. "Come undercover, have you?"

With slight hesitation the boy nodded. "Yes, Wing Commander."

"Jolly good show. I must say those Smarties worked a treat!" With that the old man winked,  and his grandson couldn't help but smile.

Grandpa had fooled them all! Then the old man looked around the room before saying, "So, Squadron Leader, how do you fancy stepping outside to do some…'gardening'?"

Jack understood exactly what this meant and winked back.

39

Bonkers

Miss Swine watched like a hawk as Grandpa and Jack disappeared out of the living room together. As families were visiting *Twilight Towers* that day, the front door was unlocked, so the pair went out and made their way across the garden. Jack's mother and father stayed inside in the warm living room, and watched them from the window.

As soon as they were a safe distance from the main building, Grandpa slipped Jack a couple of socks filled with dirt. These he was instructed to stuff down his trousers, one for each leg. As soon as they had reached the rather pitiful flower bed (which was really nothing more than a patch of earth with a couple of flower bulbs sticking out), the boy took his grandfather's lead. Waddling like a pair of penguins, first Grandpa and then Jack pulled on the elastic bands, tipping the soil socks up, and released the dirt. It trickled down their legs and out the bottom of their trousers. After checking the nurses high up on the observation towers were not looking, they patted the dirt into the soil of the flower bed with their feet.

"Was that ALL the soil from last night, Wing Commander?" asked the boy.

"Roger, Squadron Leader," replied Grandpa proudly.

Jack looked down at the tiny amount of dirt. It couldn't have been more than a few cans' worth. At this rate the tunnel wouldn't be completed until 2083.

"The thing is, erm…," the boy started a sentence, but couldn't quite finish it for fear of hurting the old man's feelings.

"Spit it out, man!" demanded Grandpa.

"Well, the thing is, I worry that the tunnel is going to take forever, if that's all the dirt you can get out in one night."

The old man looked at the boy with disdain. "Have you ever tried to dig through a stone floor armed with only a spoon?"

This answer required no real thought. Like most people on earth, Jack had never been foolish enough to attempt such a task. "No."

"Well, I don't mind telling you, it's ruddy hard going!" exclaimed Grandpa.

"So how can I help you with the escape plan, sir?"

The old man thought for a moment. "Smuggle me in a bigger spoon?"

"With respect, Wing Commander, I don't think the size of the spoon is going to make that much difference."

"I'll try anything to get out of this infernal prisoner-of-war camp. As a British officer, it is my duty to escape. You must promise to bring me another spoon tomorrow night!" demanded Grandpa.

"A soup spoon?"

"This is a mighty task, man. I need a serving spoon!"

"I promise, sir," Jack murmured.

"Squadron Leader, the only thing that keeps me going in here is the thought of getting back in my Spitfire."

At that moment, Miss Swine's suspicions must have got the better of her, as she bounded out of the building at speed. The lady tottered across the garden in her high-heeled boots, her cape flapping in the wind. Two of her sinister helpers were at her side, Nurse Rose and Nurse Blossom. They were both so big and brawny, they looked more like Matron's security guards than anything else. Trailing behind were Mum and Dad, huffing and puffing to keep up.

"On gardening duty, are we?" called Matron. Her words were riddled with distrust.

"Yes, that's right. Just tending to these flower beds, Kommandant!" shouted Grandpa.

"Kommandant?!" repeated Miss Swine. "The silly old fool thinks he is in a prisoner-of-war camp!"

Matron laughed uproariously. The two nurses were a bit slow on the uptake, but after a moment joined in with their laughter.

"HA! HA! HA!"

As Mum and Dad reached the flower bed, Miss Swine held court for a moment. "Oh, you have to have a good sense of humor to work here at Twilight Towers!"

"You certainly do, Matron," replied Nurse Rose in her gruff voice.

"So many of my old folk have gone gaga. But Grandpa here is the most gaga of them all."

"How dare you!" said the boy.

"Don't be rude to the nice matron, son," said Mum.

"Look at him!" exclaimed Matron. "This man is bonkers!"

"No, Kommandant, my name is not Bonkers, it's Bunting!" corrected Grandpa. "I think there is a Flight Lieutenant Bonkers with 501 Squadron over in Gloucester."

"Oh dear," murmured Matron. "Well, it's getting rather chilly out here, don't you think?"

"Yes, Matron," said Dad, who, being so skinny, was shivering slightly with the cold.

"Nurses? Would you be kind enough to help poor

Mr. Bunting back inside?" ordered Miss Swine.

"That's Wing Commander Bunting!" protested Grandpa.

"Yes, yes, of course it is!" replied Miss Swine sarcastically.

Together Nurse Rose and Nurse Blossom picked up the old man by his ankles. Dangling him upside down they marched back into the building.

"Let go of him!" shouted the boy.

"Do they have to carry him like that?" pleaded Dad.

"It's good for his bad back!" replied Matron cheerily.

Jack couldn't take it anymore and launched himself at one of the nurse's backs. In an instant, she swatted him away as if he were a fly.

"Jack!" exclaimed Mum, as she pulled him back by his arm.

"I won't talk, you know, Kommandant!" shouted the old man as he was carried off. "I would rather die than betray king and country!"

"Kommandant, indeed! Ho ho! That does make me giggle!" said Matron, before looking at her watch. "Well, we should all be getting back inside to enjoy the party. There's still two whole minutes of visiting time left!"

Matron ushered Mum and Dad ahead. "Please, after you, Barbara and Barry."

But then Miss Swine loitered for a moment to

have a private word with Jack. "I know you are up to something, you nasty little child…," she hissed. "I'll be watching you."

A **shiver** ran down the boy's spine.

40

A Rope of Knickers

The next evening, Jack was sat up on the top bunk in his bedroom. Under his pillow he had hidden a large serving spoon he had swiped from the school cafeteria at lunchtime. He had stuffed it down his trousers, which made him limp like he had a wooden leg.

As his model planes dangled around his head, the boy felt torn. He had promised his grandfather he would make another of his secret visits to Twilight Towers later that night. However, even with a bigger spoon, Grandpa had a less-than-zero chance of escape. The only point the boy could see of carrying on with the whole charade was so that the old man would not lose hope. Because without hope, Grandpa would have nothing. *Perhaps Grandpa could live out his days digging his tunnel, dreaming of an escape that would never come?* thought Jack. As much as he hated Twilight Towers and the sinister Miss Swine, the boy didn't have another plan. Talking to his parents again had been no use. They believed their son had an overactive imagination after spending so much time with his dotty grandfather. To them, this sounded like just another one of their fantasies.

So, regular as clockwork now, the boy waited for night to fall. Then he grabbed the serving spoon and climbed out of his bedroom window. But when he arrived at Twilight Towers, he noticed something worrying. The drainpipe that he had used before to climb up to the window of Grandpa's dormitory had been yanked off the wall. It was now lying in bits on the gravel. Were Matron and her army of nurses on to him? This was his only means of scaling the building. Frightened he would be walking into a trap that might land his grandfather in deeper trouble, the boy decided to leave immediately. But just as he was crawling back across the lawn, Jack heard a noise coming from the roof.

CREAK...

It was the sound of a little wooden door opening. Was it Miss Swine or one of her nurses? Had Jack been busted?

Looking up, he spied a figure on top of the building clambering out of a tiny hatch.

It was Grandpa!

Still in his pajamas, the old man was trying to squeeze himself through the hatch hole. The opening was small. As he forced himself through, his pajama bottoms slipped down, exposing his saggy behind.

Grandpa crawled on to the roof and stood up. As soon as he had regained his balance, he hoisted up his pajama bottoms.

The roof had quite a slope to it, and as a wicked winter wind blew across the moors, the old man wobbled on his way down to the roof edge.

Jack called up to his grandfather as quietly as he could, "What on earth are you doing up there?"

The old man looked puzzled for a moment as to where this voice was coming from.

"Down here!"

"Oh! Squadron Leader! There you are! But I think you mean, 'What on earth are you doing up there, SIR?' Let's not forget our manners, just because there is a war on."

"Apologies—what on earth are you doing up there, sir?" the boy called.

"The Kommandant suspected something was up. Had the whole camp searched from top to bottom. One of the guards found the tunnel I had dug in the basement. Well I say 'tunnel'—the scrapings on the stone floor I had made with the spoon. Now they know there is an escape afoot. Earlier, guards burst into our cells and ripped everything apart. Darn and blast them all. Smashed up furniture, upturned beds, looking for clues."

"Did they find the spoon?"

"No! I just managed to hide it by clenching it between my buttocks. It was the one place they didn't look! But I couldn't hold it there any longer. So I had to make a new plan. I escape tonight!"

"Tonight?"

"Yes, Squadron Leader."

"But, sir, how are you going to get down from there? You are four floors up."

"Yes. Shame I didn't pack my parachute. But I did manage to tie together this!" With that, the old man scuttled back to the hatch, and pulled out what looked like a rope of some sort. On closer inspection it wasn't a rope at all. In fact, it was thirty or so pairs of frilly knickers Grandpa had tied together.

"Where did you get all those knickers from, sir?"

"They're not mine, Squadron Leader. If that is what you are trying to say?!"

"No, sir!" replied the boy. Still it was an awful lot of knickers, or to use the correct term, "knickerage."

"I found them all hanging up to dry in the laundry room!" continued Grandpa. "Dozens of pairs of ladies' knickers, there were! All in extra-large sizes. Most queer!"

The old man began to uncurl his makeshift rope and let it out slowly until it reached the ground.

Oh no, thought Jack, *my elderly grandfather is going to abseil down a building using only some frilly knickers.*

"Please be careful, Grandpa, I mean Wing Commander, sir."

From his position on the ground, Jack watched as his grandfather tied his end of the rope of knickers around the bell tower at the top of Twilight Towers.

"Make sure the knot won't come undone, sir!" called up the boy.

The old RAF officer didn't appreciate being challenged like this. "I know my way around a pair of ladies' knickers, thank you very much, Squadron Leader!"

Grandpa tugged on the rope of knickers a few times to make sure it was secure. Next he held on tight with both hands, and started to lower himself down the side of the building. The silk of the knickers was surprisingly strong—it held his weight easily.

Little by little he descended to the ground.

For a moment, it looked like disaster had struck when Grandpa lost his footing. One of his slippers slipped on the wet bricks, and fell off his foot. It hit Jack on the head on the way down.

THUNK!

"Sincere apologies for that, Squadron Leader."

Jack picked up the slipper and held on to it—mightily impressed by the old man's strength and agility—until Grandpa reached the ground. The boy saluted him as he always did, and handed over his slipper as if it were a medal.

The man unbuttoned his pajamas to reveal he was wearing his blazer and slacks underneath.

"Thank you, old boy!" said Grandpa, as he pushed his foot back into his slipper.

Jack looked across the grounds of Twilight Towers. The searchlights were circling at the far end. If they moved quickly, they had a chance of not being seen and making it over the wall and to freedom.

"Right, we have to get going straightaway, sir," whispered the boy.

"Oh, yes, Squadron Leader, there is one small thing."

"What's that, Wing Commander?"

"Well, there are now quite a few of us on the escape committee."

"What do you mean, 'escape committee'?" asked Jack.

"Psst!" came a voice from above.

The pair looked up. There were a dozen or so elderly people standing on the roof. All were in their pajamas and nightdresses. More and more were joining them by the moment, as they squeezed themselves through the tiny hatch.

This was now a **mass breakout.**

41

Jolly Good Show

"Come down in an orderly fashion!" ordered Grandpa. "One at a time, please."

As the first elderly inmate abseiled down, Jack remarked, "But I thought they were all fed pills to keep them asleep."

"They were. But I shared my Smarties!"

"You did ask for rather a lot." The boy felt a wave of panic crash over him. "But how many of you are escaping tonight?"

Jack's grandpa sighed. "I hardly need to remind you, Squadron Leader, that it's every British prisoner of war's duty to escape."

"ALL OF THEM?!"

"Every last one! Put the kettle on, Mr. Churchill, we'll be home by teatime!"

As each elderly person reached the ground, Grandpa

saluted them, and they took off their nightwear to reveal their civilian clothes underneath.

 "Good evening, Major!" said Grandpa to the old gentleman sporting a ruddy nose and monocle. Jack recognized him from his visit on Sunday.

"Lovely night for a breakout, Wing Commander!" replied the man.

Grandpa saluted the next old chap to come down the rope of knickers.

"Good evening, Rear Admiral!" he said.

"Evening, Bunting. Jolly good show on the escape," replied the Rear Admiral, who once must have been very high up in the navy. He was the man from the living room the day before, the one with the hearing aid that whistled so loudly it made everyone else deaf.

"Oh, thank you, sir."

"Be sure to come and have a glass of bubbly aboard ship with me to celebrate when it's all over!"

"Be delighted to," replied Grandpa. "Good night and good luck."

"Good luck to you too. So it's this way to the wall, is it?" went on the Rear Admiral, in no apparent rush to escape.

Jack pitched in, "Yes, sir. Just climb up the overhanging branch of that willow tree, and you can get out that way."

"Right right right, I'll take a stroll over there then," replied the Rear Admiral. "See you on the other side." With that, he saluted the boy and began to light his pipe.

"Maybe wait until you are over the wall until you smoke your pipe, sir?" suggested Jack. "You don't want to attract the searchlights."

"No no no. Of course not. Silly of me!" agreed the old chap, as he put the pipe back in his pocket and stepped out into the darkness.

Suddenly something of an uproar was coming from the roof. The final escapee, the large lady Jack had spied yesterday in the living room, had become stuck in the hatch. Now she was calling down for help.

"I am stuck, Wing Commander!" she cried.

"Oh no!" sighed Grandpa. "It's Trifle. She must be one of the WAAFS."

"Women's Auxiliary Air Force?" replied the boy.

"Yes, but instead of mapping out positions of enemy aircraft, she has been at the cakes! I should have known she wouldn't make it through that little hatch. Squadron Leader, you stay here. I am going back up!" he announced.

"No, sir!" replied Jack defiantly. "It's too dangerous. I am coming with you!"

Grandpa smiled at the younger man. "That's the spirit, Squadron Leader!"

With that, the pair began climbing back up the rope of knickers to the roof.

"It's much harder going up!" said the old man.

By now the knickerage had been stretched to very nearly breaking point.

Seeing all the rips in the silk on the way up, Jack wasn't convinced it was going to take Mrs. Trifle's weight on the way down. But there was no plan B. They would have to try.

Finally the pair managed to hoist themselves up onto the roof.

Jack and his grandfather stood looking at stuck Mrs. Trifle and pondered what to do.

"One arm each, I think," said Grandpa confidently, as if he was an expert on extracting large women from small hatches.

"This is most undignified!" announced the elderly lady. Mrs. Trifle was frightfully posh. "And I need to use the *powder room.*"

"The what?" asked Jack.

"The, um, *convenience,*" replied the lady.

"The what?" The boy had no idea what she was talking about.

"The, erm, um, *the commode!*"

"Sorry, I don't know what you are talking about!"

"I AM BURSTING FOR THE BOG!" shouted Mrs. Trifle angrily.

"Oh, sorry…"

"It will have to wait a moment, Trifle," said Grandpa. "First, we have to get you out of this hatch."

"Yes! If you wouldn't mind!" Her tone was sarcastic, as if it was all Grandpa's fault. It certainly wasn't his fault that the lady had spent a lifetime eating cake. But there was no time to get into all that now.

"If only we could get someone up the rear end to push!" mused the old man.

"Oh, charming!" complained the posh lady loudly. "You make me sound like a broken-down bus!"

"If you could keep it down, please, madam!" whispered Grandpa. "You will alert the guards."

"I won't say another word!" replied Mrs. Trifle. Still a little too loudly for Jack's and Grandpa's liking.

"Ready, Squadron Leader?" asked the old man.

"Ready, sir," replied the boy.

Grandpa and Jack took an arm each.

"Take the strain, Squadron Leader," said

Grandpa. "Now, on three, heave. One, two, three, HEAVE!"

Nothing.

The lady did not budge an inch.

"This is not my idea of a nice night out!" said Mrs. Trifle, helping nobody.

"Again!" ordered Grandpa. "One, two, three, HEAVE!"

Still nothing.

"Next time someone asks me to join them on an escape, please remind me to *politely decline!*" muttered the lady, mainly to herself. "I only said yes for the free Smarties."

"One last go!" announced Grandpa. "One, two, three, HEAVE!"

This time, somehow, Mrs. Trifle managed to slide down the hatch back into Twilight Towers.

"*Well, thank you very much!*" complained the old dear. "Now I'll be stuck here forever!"

"What on earth are we going to do, sir?" pleaded Jack. "We are never going to get her free, and time is running out!"

42

Bruises on the Bottom

"I am thinking, Squadron Leader," said Grandpa as they stood on the roof of Twilight Towers. "I don't want to leave a single man…"

"Or lady!" corrected Mrs. Trifle.

"…or lady behind. We need backup. Let me call on the army and navy." With that, Grandpa scuttled over to the edge of the roof and called out into the darkness below, "Major? Rear Admiral?"

"Yes, sir?" came the voice of the Major from on the ground.

"I need reinforcements!"

Without hesitation, the two old war heroes made their way back across the lawn and up the rope of knickers. They were followed one by one by a dozen or so of the other escapees.

"Would you mind hurrying up, please?" complained Mrs. Trifle. "I do need to use the loo!"

The old folk joined together to form two human chains. At the end of each chain someone held on tight to one of Mrs. Trifle's arms.

"Teamwork!" announced Grandpa. "That's what will win us this war. Teamwork! We all need to work together."

"Hear hear!" agreed the major.

Next, Grandpa called out his command. "One, two, three, HEAVE!"

This time Mrs. Trifle shot up through the hatch. In an instant, everyone flew backward to end up piled on top of each other in a heap.

OOF!

"Teamwork, sir!" remarked Jack with a smile, as he climbed out from the bottom of the pile.

"Bravo, one and all!" said Grandpa. "Right, now everyone back down the rope quick smart."

One by one the other old folk made their way back down. Mrs. Trifle was the last in line.

Surveying her for a second, Jack whispered, "I am not sure the rope will take her weight, sir."

"I checked, and rest assured they are all top-quality British-made knickers, Squadron Leader. I am sure everything will be fine if Trifle just listens to my instructions and takes it slow…"

Mrs. Trifle was not one to listen to instructions from anybody. Without waiting, she grabbed hold of the knickerage and launched herself off the roof with far too much gusto. Just as Jack had predicted, the rope could not take her weight. As she slid down it at alarming speed…

"AAAAAARRRRRGGGGGHHHHH!"

…a pair of the silky knickers RIPPED.

RiP!

And Mrs. Trifle landed on the ground.

Thud!

"OOOOOOOOOOOOOOOOWW WWWWWWWWWWWWWWWWW WWWW!" she screamed.

Fortunately she did not fall too far and was not badly injured. Just a few bruises on her bottom. The rope of knickers followed her down and landed on top of her head.

"Now I am covered in knickers!" she complained loudly. "I can never show my face in polite society again!"

"Shush!" shushed Jack.

But it was too late. The nurses stationed atop the observation towers could not help but hear the very loud Mrs. Trifle. Immediately the searchlights circled. One picked out Mrs. Trifle, another the gaggle of elderly escapees hurrying across the lawn.

"Quick! Run for the willow tree!"

Jack called down from the roof. "It's your only way out!" Helping each other as much as they could, the old folk surged toward the wall.

Suddenly a blinding blaze of lights lit up the building and all its grounds.

DING DONG DING DONG DING DONG DING DONG!

The bell in the tower began to ring. The alarm had been raised.

One of the searchlights caught Grandpa and Jack on the roof. For a moment they were framed in the glare of a light. With the rope of knickers broken, there was no way down.

They were trapped.

43

Down the Hatch

Jack and his grandfather watched from the roof of Twilight Towers, as the elderly escapees disappeared over the perimeter wall.

"Good luck, men," muttered the old man, giving them one last salute before they vanished from view.

They were being chased by a gang of nurses who had rushed out of the building in pursuit, carrying torches and huge nets.

Meanwhile, Jack and his grandfather were four floors up. The rope of knickers had ripped. The drainpipe had been yanked off the wall. If they tried to jump, they would surely break every bone in their bodies. Jack could only see one way out. "Down the hatch, sir!"

"Oh, is it cocktail hour?" asked Grandpa innocently. "I'll have a gin and tonic, please."

"No, I mean we have to go down the hatch. It's the only way out!"

"Oh, yes, of course. Good thinking, Squadron Leader. I must recommend you to the Air Chief Marshal for a medal!"

The boy thought he would burst with pride. "Thank you, sir. But there's no time to lose! Let's go!"

Jack took his grandfather's hand to guide him across the sloping roof. One slip and they could plummet to their deaths. But just as they reached the hatch, they spotted the end of Matron's baton snaking out of it. The end fizzed with electricity. Jack suddenly realized it was in fact a cattle prod used by farmers to give cows an electric shock to move them in the right direction. But in the matron's hands it must be some kind of instrument of torture.

The little lady crawled out of the hatch and rose to her feet. As she stood on the roof, she held the cattle prod aloft, her cape billowing in the wind.

One by one Nurses Rose and Blossom forced their bulky bodies through the hatch too, and joined her.

With a sinister smile on her face the wicked lady
edged forward, a nurse on either side.

"I knew you two were up to no good in the garden
yesterday," she purred. "There has been a mass escape
tonight, and you are the ringleaders!"

"Don't punish him, please. I beg you!" pleaded Jack. "The escape was all my idea!"

"Actually, Kommandant, it's me you should be sending to the punishment block. This young chap here had absolutely nothing to do with the plan!"

"SILENCE!" she shouted. "Both of you!"

And there was silence.

Matron pressed the button on her cattle prod and a huge bolt of electricity shot out of the end.

"What are you going to do with that, Kommandant?" asked Grandpa.

"I had this cattle prod specially modified to have ten million volts passing through it! Enough to knock a grown man out cold with just one press of this button."

Grandpa moved his grandson behind him protectively. "That's barbaric, Kommandant!" he exclaimed. "The use of torture is forbidden on prisoners of war!"

A manic smile spread over Miss Swine's face. "Just you watch me." With that she poked Nurse Rose with the cattle prod and pressed the button. A white-

and-blue bolt leaped off its end.

For a moment the nurse's entire body was lit up by electricity. Matron took her finger off the button and the nurse fell to the floor unconscious.

As Miss Swine chuckled to herself, Jack and his grandfather looked on in stunned silence. How could she do that to one of her own henchwomen? Even Nurse Blossom appeared nervous, and shifted uncomfortably on her feet.

"Sorry, I just need to see that one more time," ventured Grandpa. The old man was betting on the matron falling for his ruse, and taking out the other nurse as well.

"I am not falling for that, old man!" announced Matron. Nurse Blossom breathed a sigh of relief.

"Grab them!" ordered Miss Swine.

The burly nurse stepped over her unconscious colleague and surged forward. With her thick arms outstretched, she made a lunge at them.

"The bell tower!" cried Grandpa.

Twilight Towers's bell was still ringing to sound the alarm. As they got closer, the noise became deafening. The bell was suspended in a little turret; beneath it was a long, thick rope.

"GRAB HOLD OF THE ROPE!" shouted the old man. The problem

was the rope was moving up and down rapidly, as someone below tugged on it to ring the bell.

Jack looked over his shoulder to see Nurse Blossom advancing on them. Miss Swine was close behind, brandishing her cattle prod. There was no choice. Jack took a leap and seized the rope with both hands. Immediately he felt as if his palms were on fire as he slid down the shaft at great speed.

"Argh!" cried the boy.

Jack looked down and saw it was Nurse Daisy below him, swinging on the rope. Just as she looked up, Jack crashed down on top of her.

Bash!

The nurse broke his fall AND was knocked out cold in the process. *RESULT!* thought the boy. But as Nurse Daisy splayed on the floor, her wig came off, revealing a shaved head underneath. On closer inspection, the nurse had stubble all over her face too.

She was a man!

44

All Sorts

Standing at the bottom of the bell tower, Jack heard a noise above his head. Looking up, he saw Grandpa coming down the rope at quite a speed. The boy quickly stepped aside, out of the old man's way.

"Look, Wing Commander, she's a man!" said the boy as Grandpa landed. Now it made sense why the nurses at Twilight Towers were so big and burly. "Maybe they all are!"

Grandpa peered down at the man. "Oh well, it takes all sorts, I suppose. I trained with an excellent pilot named Charles. At the weekends, he would dress up and tell us all to call him Clarissa. Made an extremely pretty woman. Had one or two marriage proposals."

Sadly there wasn't time to properly process this fascinating snippet of information. Right now, they

had to find some way out of Twilight Towers.
Grandpa knew the inside of the building much better
than Jack. "Where to next, Wing Commander?" the
boy asked.

"I am thinking, Squadron Leader, I am thinking…"
said the old man.

But before Grandpa had a chance to do so, the boy
cried, **"Look out!"**

Jack yanked his grandfather out of the way as
Nurse Blossom hurtled down with her—or perhaps
rather *his*—very hairy legs wrapped around the
rope.

"Quick! This way!" said Grandpa, as the
pair hurried off.

Just as Nurse Daisy was coming to, Nurse Blossom
landed on top of her, knocking her out cold again.

Bash!

In the collision, Nurse
Blossom's wig came off
too. She was also a
man! *All the nurses at*

Twilight Towers *must be*, thought Jack. Nothing at this old folk's home was as it seemed.

As the bald heavy scrambled to his feet, Jack and his grandfather reached the door. It was open and they quickly slammed it shut behind them.

SLAM!

As Nurse Blossom (or whatever his real name was) pounded on the door with his fists that were heavy as bricks, Jack and Grandpa forced their backs

up against it. The "nurse" was as strong as a bull, and they couldn't hold him back for much longer.

"The sideboard, Squadron Leader!" ordered Grandpa.

The old man kept his back against the door and his grandson

pushed the heavy wooden piece of furniture into place in front of it, trapping Nurse Blossom and Nurse Daisy in the bell tower.

The door began to slam against the sideboard…

SLAM! SLAM! SLAM!

…and the pair dashed down the long corridor toward the front door. Just then, the sound of footsteps echoed down the stairs. It was a platoon of more "nurses," no doubt on their way to search for the escapees.

"They're everywhere," whispered Jack, as he and his grandpa hid on the other side of a grandfather clock while the "nurses" passed. "We'll never be able to sneak out now, sir!" said the boy.

"Well, in that case…I learned this at training camp!" announced the old man. "Our only hope of escape is to disguise ourselves as them."

Jack wasn't sure he had quite understood what Grandpa had just said.

"You mean…"

"Yes, Squadron Leader. We must put on their uniforms."

45

Wigs and Makeup

As they stepped out of the changing room, Jack and his grandfather made an unlikely pair of nurses. The boy was unusually short and there wasn't time for Grandpa to shave off his bushy mustache.

The changing room was situated at the back of the old folk's home and had a long rail of nurses' uniforms. Jack and Grandpa had hastily grabbed a couple and put them on over their own clothes. At the far end of the changing rooms stood a tall mirror, and a table with a selection of wigs and a big box of makeup that Jack and his grandfather had raided. Grandpa had become a blond bombshell, his grandson a sultry brunette.

The boy was right; the nurses were clearly all men in disguise. Twilight Towers was certainly no ordinary old folk's home. Each time you peeled off a layer, it became stranger and stranger.

As they tottered down the corridor, a group of "nurses" bundled past, charging toward the front door. Grandpa nodded to Jack that they should join them. Their only chance of escape now was to try and blend in with the staff. They had to pray that they would not get stopped as they made their way along the labyrinth of corridors toward freedom.

As the "nurses" reached the front door, Grandpa and Jack followed a short distance behind. But just as they were about to escape out into the dark, a voice bellowed. **"STOP!"**

All the "nurses" turned around to see Matron standing behind them, still wielding her souped-up cattle prod. Nurses Daisy and Blossom were flanking her. These two now had their wigs on back to front and they both looked even more ridiculous than before. Matron approached her army of "nurses" slowly, gently tapping the palm of her hand with her instrument of torture.

As discreetly as they could, Jack and his grandfather shuffled themselves to the back of the group so as not to be seen by her.

"The rest of our inmates seem to have got away. For now. But the two ringleaders of tonight's breakout are still here in *Twilight Towers*. I am sure of it," Miss Swine announced. "I can feel it in my bones. And they are the ones who must not escape."

"Yes, Matron," came a chorus of voices, all far too deep to be women.

"My orders are for you all to split up into pairs, and search every last nook and cranny of this building until you find them. If you fail, I will turn my cattle prod on you!" she shouted.

"Y-y-y-yes, Matron." Despite all the "nurses" being big strong men, it was clear they lived in mortal fear of their boss.

With great authority, she barked further orders to her troops. "Nurses Tulip and Hyacinth, search the dormitories."

"Yes, Matron," they answered, before marching off toward the stairs.

"Nurses Violet and Pansy? You two search this floor, the living room, the kitchen. Everywhere."

"Yes, Matron," replied the next pair before they marched off too.

"Nurses Daisy and Blossom?"

"Yes, Matron?" they answered in unison.

"You can search the basement."

"But I am scared of the dark!" complained Nurse Daisy.

Miss Swine's face contorted in displeasure. She was not used to having her orders disobeyed. She slapped the palm of her hand hard with her cattle prod. "You will do as I say!"

"Yes, Matron!" replied the nervy "nurse," now trembling in fear.

The pair headed off.

That left Matron alone in the corridor with her newest "nurses," Jack and Grandpa.

"As for you…" Miss Swine was looking straight at them. The pair had no one to hide behind now.

The boy was standing on his tiptoes in an attempt to look taller. Meanwhile his grandfather was covering his mustache with his hand and pretending to cough.

"I haven't seen you two here before. Who are you?!" demanded Miss Swine.

Jack put on his deepest voice. "Nurses, Matron."

"What are your names?"

The pair had to think fast if they were not going to get busted.

"Nurse Bluebell!" replied Jack.

"And Nurse Graham," said Grandpa, forgetting he was meant to choose a girl's name.

Jack gently jabbed him with his elbow. "I mean Gardenia!"

Slowly and calmly Matron approached them. Both instinctively put their heads down in a desperate attempt not to be recognized. This made Matron even more suspicious. Still tapping the prod in her hand she stepped closer and closer.

"Take your hand away from your face," she whispered to the old man.

Grandpa pretended to cough again. "Bit of a cold coming on!"

The lady brought her hand up to his. She held on to it tight, digging her long, sharp nails into his skin. Then with considerable force she pulled his hand down from his face, revealing his RAF standard-issue mustache.

"Just forgot to pluck today," Grandpa tried.

Needless to say, Matron was not convinced. Slowly but surely, she brought up her prod and moved it toward the old man's face. As she did so a bolt of electricity shot out of the end.

Grandpa gulped in terror.

GULP!

46

Burned Mustache

"Excuse me! I just need to use the convenience," announced Mrs. Trifle just at that moment. As she spoke she strode in through the front door behind Grandpa and Jack. Instead of escaping over the wall with all the other inmates, it seemed the old lady had done a U-turn and waltzed straight back into Twilight Towers in search of the loo. This was certainly not part of the plan, but it proved an excellent diversion, just when Jack and his grandfather desperately needed one.

Miss Swine turned her head to see Mrs. Trifle breeze through the front door. With Matron's cattle prod inches from his face, Grandpa seized the opportunity and grabbed the woman's wrist. For a moment, the two were locked in a silent wrestle. The lady was much stronger than the old man could ever

have imagined, and the end of the prod moved closer and closer to his face. Suddenly a bolt of electricity shot out.

It burned one end of his mustache off.

In a fizzle of flames, a small plume of gray smoke rose past Grandpa's eyes. He looked down at his once magnificent facial hair. Now one side was nothing more than a blackened tip, like a sausage that had been left on the barbecue for a hundred years. The blackened tip then crumbled, and fell to the floor as dust.

Ever since he was a young man, Grandpa had prided himself on looking immaculate—even in a nurse's uniform. But the double-breasted blazer with polished gold buttons, the RAF tie, the neatly pressed gray slacks, all amounted to nothing if his mustache wasn't perfectly twizzled.

For Grandpa, for one end of his mustache to be burned off was treason. The fury he felt gave the old man an almost superhuman surge of strength. He forced the woman's arm back toward her.

"Squadron Leader, grab that bedpan, quick!" he ordered.

Jack picked up the porcelain pot from the floor, and in his confusion went to offer it to Mrs. Trifle.

"Thank you, dear," said the old lady. "It's not ideal

but if I can aim straight I can make do!"

"No, Squadron Leader! Use it on the Kommandant!"

Matron spun around, just as the boy lifted the bedpan above his head and crashed it down on hers.

SMASH!!

The pot exploded into hundreds of tiny pieces.

"Well, thank you very much!" complained Mrs. Trifle. "I was all ready to go." The three looked down at the evil woman, now lying on the carpet spread out like a starfish.

"There's no time to lose!" barked Grandpa.

"Can I PLEASE just have my tinkle?" demanded Mrs. Trifle.

"Trifle—pull yourself together, woman! It will have to wait!" Grandpa ordered.

"You can't wait when you

get to my age!" huffed the elderly lady. "When you need to go, you need to go! Now please, escort me! I thought you were a gentleman?"

"I am a gentleman!" exclaimed Grandpa, though his gentlemanliness was being tested to the limit.

"Then why are you dressed like that?" the old lady inquired.

"It's all part of the escape plan!" snapped Grandpa. "Now please, madam, there is no time to lose, take my arm."

"Thank you, Wing Commander. My poor... erm... what is the polite word?" She pointed to her behind.

"Bottom?" ventured Grandpa.

"No!" said Mrs. Trifle.

"Bum!" said the boy cheekily.

"NO!" Mrs. Trifle was quite cross now. "I am a lady! I was going to say posterior! My poor posterior is awfully sore after that fall. I can hardly walk in a straight line!"

With her arm in his, Grandpa gallantly

accompanied the elderly lady down the long corridor and round the corner to the nearest lavatory.

"Oh, what a gentleman! I feel like a debutante at her first society ball!" Mrs. Trifle blushed.

"Squadron Leader?" called out Grandpa.

"Yes, sir?"

"You keep an eye on the Kommandant!"

"Yes, sir!" replied the boy with a smile. Although shaking with nerves, he was rather pleased with himself to have been the one to deliver the knockout blow to the evil Miss Swine.

Jack peered down at her. The face looked strangely familiar with those little eyes and upturned nose. But before Jack had time to think about where he might have seen her before, Miss Swine began to flicker back to life. The bedpan had knocked her out all right, but now she was slowly coming to. First her fingers began to twitch, and then her eyes began to blink.

The boy felt a deep sense of **dread**.

47

Shake & Go

"Wing Commander!" Jack called down the corridor, a note of panic creeping into his voice.

"Go ahead, Squadron Leader," came Grandpa's voice from around the corner.

"The Kommandant is beginning to come to, sir!"

The next sound Jack heard was his grandfather knocking on the toilet door.

KNOCK KNOCK.

"Will you hurry up in there, Trifle?!"

"Never rush a lady on the lavatory!" barked Mrs. Trifle from inside.

"Please, madam!" ordered Grandpa.

"I have waited long enough for this, I am going to enjoy it, thank you very much!"

Just then the boy noticed that the matron's limbs were snaking into life too.

"Sir!" he called out in desperation.

The old man tried once again to hurry the lady up.

KNOCK KNOCK KNOCK.

"Finished!" she finally answered from the other side of the toilet door. "Typical! There's no paper. Would you be a darling and find me some? The absorbent kind, please, I can't abide the shiny white!"

"There's no time, Trifle." Grandpa was trying to be polite but from his tone of voice it was clear he was becoming increasingly irritated with the old lady now.

"What do you expect me to do?" complained Mrs. Trifle.

"Just shake and go! That's what us men do!"

There was silence for a short while, before Mrs. Trifle announced in a cheery tone, "Why, thank you! That's actually done the trick."

The boy turned to see the two elderly escapees finally reappearing around the corner. Suddenly Grandpa shouted, "Squadron Leader! LOOK OUT!"

Jack spun around. Matron was now scrabbling

to her feet, and reaching out the prod in the boy's direction.

"RUN!" shouted Grandpa.

Miss Swine lunged her weapon at Jack like a sword, electric bolts shooting from the tip. Sparks flew on to the thick velvet curtains behind him. Immediately they were set alight, and flames licked the ceiling.

48

Inferno!

To escape the flames, Jack backed down the corridor. He reached Grandpa and Mrs. Trifle. Together the three hurried away from the fire. Matron staggered after them, her body framed by the oncoming inferno. The flames were moving fast, and soon they were catching up with her.

"ARGH!" cried Miss Swine at the blazing heat.

The fire was rapidly becoming out of control, devouring everything in sight. Flames leaped along the corridor in front of her. In an instant, Miss Swine had become trapped by the blaze.

"You take care of Trifle, old boy," ordered Grandpa. "I should save the Kommandant!"

"What?" Jack couldn't believe his ears.

"They may be my enemy, but as an officer and

a gentleman it is a matter of honor—I must try and save the Kommandant!"

With that, the old man shielded his face from the flames with his arm, and walked bravely toward Miss Swine.

"Kommandant!" he said. "Give me your hand!"

He stretched out his arm through the flames.

Miss Swine reached out her hand to meet his. She grabbed it tight, and smiled craftily at the old man.

"Take this, you gibbering old fool!" she cried, as she lifted her cattle prod high into the air.

"WATCH OUT!" cried the boy.

Bash!

It was too late.

Miss Swine had walloped Grandpa over the head with her cattle prod, knocking him unconscious to the ground.

"Noooo!" cried Jack.

49

Hot as Hell

A crazed smile crossed Miss Swine's face. It now looked like she was going in for the kill. But as she violently swung her cattle prod up in the air to zap Grandpa this time, she lost her balance on her high heels. Matron toppled backward into the flames, screaming. "AAAAAARRRRRRRRRR RRRGGGGGGGGGG GGHHHHHHHHH HH!!!!!"

Jack rushed forward and dragged his poor grandfather from the path of the inferno.

Their only way out of the building was the front door, and that was now blocked by the blaze. As the boy had already discovered, the back doorway of **Twilight Towers** had been bricked up and there were bars on all the windows. The place was a death trap.

Thick black smoke was now billowing along the corridor. It was rapidly becoming as hot as hell.

Jack took a deep breath. He needed to find some way out of **Twilight Towers**. And fast. Now he had two elderly people in his care. His grandfather, who had been knocked out, and a posh old lady who was rapidly getting on his nerves.

Holding Grandpa's ankles under his arms, he pulled him to where Mrs. Trifle was waiting a safe distance from the flames.

"Well, I must say," began the old lady, "this place has really gone off!"

"Will you help me?" pleaded the boy. "Take a leg!"

For once Mrs. Trifle did what she was told. "May

I inquire as to where we are going?"

"Anywhere! Away from the fire!" yelled the boy.

Together they dragged the old man along the corridor and up the huge flight of stairs.

It was hard going, and poor Grandpa's head bumped on
each step.

BUMP

BUMP

BUMP.

"Ow! Ow! Ow!" he murmured at regular intervals.

The upside was, it was waking the old man up, and by the time they had reached the first floor he had opened his eyes again.

"Are you all right, sir?" asked the boy as he bent down over him.

"Yes. Just a nasty bump on my head. Next time I try to save the Kommandant, please stop me!"

"Will do, sir!" replied Jack, taking off his nurse's uniform to reveal his own clothes underneath.

"Excuse me," said Mrs. Trifle, tapping the boy on the shoulder, "how do you propose we get out of this dreadful place?"

"I don't know yet!" snapped the boy. In his mind he flicked through all the rooms in Twilight Towers he had seen when he had first climbed up the drainpipe a few nights ago. Suddenly Jack had an idea so crazy that it might just work.

320

"Sir, do you still have the roller skates I gave you the other night?" he said.

"Yes," replied Grandpa quizzically, as he rose to his feet, ripping off his own nurse's uniform.

"Can you get them?" asked the boy urgently.

"Yes, of course. They are in my dormitory. I hid them in my mattress."

"Then grab them right away, sir! And the string! And you know where the matron...I mean the Kommandant's office is?"

"Of course, Squadron Leader."

"There's some top secret, er...Nazi documents piled up on the desk! Take everything in sight. Then meet us in the room at the end of this landing," Jack said, pointing to it.

"Roger that!"

As Grandpa dashed off down the landing, Mrs. Trifle looked at the boy in astonishment. "Child, this isn't the time to go skate—" It was as if she was about to say "skate-boarding" and only realized she had gone wrong mid-word. "—rollering."

"Roller-skating?" corrected the boy.

"That's what I said!" harrumphed the lady.

"No! I have a better idea! Follow me!"

Jack ushered Mrs. Trifle along the landing to the last door at the end. Just as the boy had remembered, this was the spookiest room of all in Twilight Towers.

The room of coffins.

"Oh my goodness!" The old lady gasped in shock at the sight of the rows and rows of wooden boxes. "I always suspected that all the awful matron and her ghastly nurses were doing was waiting for us to die. I know I am old, but there's life in this old girl yet!"

The boy shut the door behind them to keep the smoke out, and then approached Mrs. Trifle. Her eyes were glazed with tears, and Jack rested a comforting hand on her shoulder.

"We are going to get out of here, Mrs. Trifle. I promise you," whispered the boy.

The door swung open. It was Grandpa proudly holding the roller skates, a ball of string, and a pile of the wills from Matron's office. The old man saluted and the boy saluted back. Over his grandson's shoulder, Grandpa spied the coffins for the first time.

"For goodness' sake, man, what on earth are we doing in here?" he thundered.

Jack gathered his thoughts for a moment. "Raj told me the only way out of Twilight Towers was in a coffin…"

"I don't follow," replied the old lady.

"Spit it out, man!" said Grandpa.

"Well, I think he was right. That's how we are going to get out of here. In one of those…"

50

Coffboggan

"That is preposterous!" announced Mrs. Trifle grandly.

"With respect, madam, I think the Squadron Leader is on to something!" replied Grandpa.

"Thank you, sir!" said the boy. "If we're lucky, a high-speed coffin should protect us from the flames for just long enough. We just need to find the largest one, and fasten the roller skates to the bottom of it with the string."

Mrs. Trifle harrumphed again—she was quite a harrumpher—but joined in the search. Working as a team, the three had soon found the largest coffin. Then as fast as they could they tied the roller skates to the underside with the string. Next the three lifted the coffin off its stand, and placed it on the floor.

Jack rolled it to and fro, and Grandpa smiled. He

had taught the young boy well—this was a quite brilliant plan.

As soon as Jack opened the door, he could feel the intense heat from the fire. Thick black smoke was now billowing everywhere. In haste, the three wheeled the coffin out on to the landing. When they reached the stairs, they saw a huge wall of flames at the bottom, waiting to swallow them up. They were running out of time. Fast.

"Mrs. Trifle?" began Jack.

"Yes, dear?"

"You lie down in here first, please."

"Oh, this is most undignified!" she complained, but did what she was told and clambered into the contraption. Jack kept the heavy lid under his arm, then gave the order.

"Right, Wing Commander, full throttle, please!"

"Roger!" replied Grandpa.

The two unlikely heroes ran alongside this coffin on wheels, gathering as much speed as they could. **It was as if the coffin was a toboggan. A coffin toboggan. A coffboggan.** As they were about to reach the top of the stairs, the pair leaped in behind Mrs. Trifle. Jack first. Then Grandpa. The old lady shrieked as the coffboggan thumped down the stairs at speed…

"Argh!"

"Aarrgghh!!"

BONK

BONK   BONK

...heading straight into the mouth of the inferno.
Jack pulled the lid in place over them and held it tight.

Inside the coffboggan, it was now pitch-black. As it bumped and banged, first down the staircase, then along the downstairs corridors, the three felt a sudden surge of intense heat.

It was HOT HOT HOT.

For a moment, it was as if they were three joints of meat roasting in an oven.

Then…

CRASH!!

…the coffboggan smashed straight through the front door.

BOOM!

Jack's plan had worked like a dream.

YES!

All of a sudden the sound of the wheels rolling on the ground changed. The crunching noise meant that they were now trundling along the gravel path outside. They had made it!

The coffboggan ground to an abrupt halt. The boy pushed the lid off. Immediately he noticed the once-brown coffin was now completely black with soot.

Jack leaped out, before helping his grandfather and finally Mrs. Trifle up.

The front gates of Twilight Towers were still shut, so the boy ushered the elderly pair across the lawn in the direction of the overhanging willow tree. He helped the two old folk first, and then climbed up himself. Standing on the tree's branch, Jack and his grandfather looked back at Twilight Towers for one last time. They had escaped not a moment too soon.

The entire building was being devoured by the fire. Flames shot out of the exploding windows, licking the outside walls. Even the roof was now ablaze.

Just before they turned to go Jack said, "Congratulations, sir. You did it!"

Grandpa looked down at his grandson. "No. WE did it!"

In the distance, Jack could see all the "nurses" fleeing across the fields. As for Miss Swine, she was absolutely nowhere to be seen. Had she remained trapped in the burning building? Or had she somehow escaped too?

Something told Jack that he had not seen the last of her.

51

Swoon

The trio looked like a circus act on the boy's trike. It was designed for one very small child, not one rather large child and two elderly people. After trying out a number of positions, they finally managed to arrange themselves. Jack was on the seat of the trike pedaling, Mrs. Trifle balanced her bottom on the handlebars, and Grandpa stood at the back on the rear frame.

Because of Mrs. Trifle's enormous bulk, Jack couldn't see a thing. Her ample bottom was pushed right up against the poor boy's face. Instead, Grandpa had to shout out directions as they trundled off down the country lane toward the town.

"Right turn, forty degrees! Oncoming milk float at three o'clock."

The plan was to head straight to the police station. Armed with the bundle of forged wills (or the top secret "Nazi documents") Grandpa had stolen, the country would finally learn the ugly truth about Twilight Towers and the wicked lady who had run the place—whether she was ever found or not. If the "nurses" could be caught, they too would all be looking at a lifetime behind bars for their evil deeds.

It was hard going on the trike, especially uphill, and by the time the three finally arrived at the local police station it was the early hours of the morning. The town was completely deserted. After Jack and his grandfather's previous misadventure with the police, the boy decided that Mrs. Trifle should be the one to go in and present the bundle of evidence, or as Grandpa believed, the secret enemy plans being turned over to British Intelligence.

"Well, good-bye, Mrs. Trifle!" said Jack. As much as she had gotten on his nerves, he was going to miss her.

"Good-bye, young man," said the old lady. "It was quite a night. I am not sure I will ever dance *Giselle* again, but thank you."

"Well, good-bye, Trifle," said Grandpa.

"Farewell, Wing Commander," she replied coquettishly.

As she closed her eyes and puckered up for a long lingering kiss, Grandpa looked a little shy.

He gave the lady a peck on the cheek, and even that made her swoon. It was clear she was holding a candle for this war hero.

As they watched her go inside the police station,

Jack turned to his grandfather. "Well, sir, it's very late. I should get you home."

"Oh no no no, Squadron Leader." Grandpa chuckled at the very thought.

"What do you mean 'no'?" asked the boy.

"By 'no' I mean 'no'! In case you had forgotten, Squadron Leader, there is a war on!"

"But—"

"Any moment now the Luftwaffe could launch another offensive. I must return to active duty at once."

"Shouldn't you at least have a lie-down, sir? A quick forty winks?" suggested Jack in desperation.

"Where is your sense of adventure, man? We must go back to base and take my Spitfire out of the hangar!"

"What?"

Grandpa looked up to the early-morning clouds.

The boy followed his gaze.

"We must take to the skies at once!" exclaimed the old man.

52

Lost Marbles

No.

It was impossible.

The Spitfire was miles away in London, suspended from the ceiling of the Imperial War Museum. She was an antique and hadn't flown for years. Who knew if she still could?

The boy had to think fast if he was to head this off at the pass. "Wing Commander?"

"Yes, Squadron Leader?"

"Let me just get Air Chief Marshal on the blower."

As Grandpa looked on, the boy opened the door of the red telephone box that stood outside the police station. Of course Jack had no idea of the number of the Air Chief Marshal. Instead, he tricked his grandfather by calling the Speaking Clock. It was an easy number to remember: 123.

With the door ajar for Grandpa's benefit, he proceeded to have an imaginary conversation with the head of the RAF. In 1940.

"Ah! Good morning, Air Chief Marshal. It's Squadron Leader Bunting. Yes, it is very late, or very early, depending on how you look at it! Ha-ha!" The boy had never been in a school play, but now was having to act as convincingly as he could.

On the other end of the line the recorded voice spoke in Jack's ear.

"At the third stroke it will be two o'clock precisely," followed by, "Beep. Beep. Beep."

Standing outside, Grandpa was mightily impressed that this young pilot knew their superior so well that they could share a joke together.

"I am with Wing Commander Bunting. Yes,

sir. That's right, your bravest pilot…"

The old man was overcome with pride.

"Some wonderful news, Air Chief Marshal!" continued Jack. "The Wing Commander has escaped from Colditz Castle! Yes, of course, it was an incredibly daring escape. He helped every last soldier, sailor, airwoman, and airman out of that darned place. What's that, sir? You say the Wing Commander needs

to rest and recuperate? Take some well-earned leave?"

Suddenly Grandpa's expression changed. This he did not like one bit.

"And that's an order, sir? Don't you worry, Air Chief Marshal, I can tell him myself," said Jack down the phone to the Speaking Clock. "So you are saying the Wing Commander should do a spot of gardening? Read a good book? Bake the odd cake?"

Grandpa was not a man who

could live out his days baking cakes.

"Good grief! There's a war on! I need to get back in my Spitfire at once! It's my duty! Let me speak to the Air Chief Marshal!"

With that Grandpa snatched the handset from his grandson.

"Sir? It's Wing Commander Bunting here."

"On the third stroke the time will be two-oh-one and forty seconds," came the voice on the other end of the line.

"What's that, Air Chief Marshal? Yes, I know the time! You don't have to keep telling me the time! Sir? Sir?"

The old man was mightily confused, and replaced the receiver before turning to Jack. "Sorry to say the Air Chief Marshal has completely lost his marbles! The man just kept on telling me the blasted time!"

"Let me call him again!" pleaded Jack, a note of desperation in his voice.

"No, no, no! There is no time. We must go *Up, up, and away!*"

PART III

ONE OF OUR AIRCRAFT IS MISSING

53

Glory Days

Jack managed to convince his grandfather that before they went "Up, up, and away" they needed to stop off for some rations. It was the early hours of the morning and Jack knew there would only be one shop open. Raj's Newsagent. In truth, the boy hoped the newsagent might be able to talk some sense into the old man.

DING!

It was still early, but Raj stood behind his counter. He was sorting through the pile of newspapers for delivery, as he did every morning.

"Mr. Bumting! You're back!" remarked the newsagent. He couldn't quite believe his eyes. After witnessing the old man being carted off to Twilight Towers by Miss Swine herself, he wasn't expecting to see Grandpa again anytime soon.

"Yes, Char Wallah! Escaped from Jerry!" announced the old man.

"Jerry who?" asked Raj.

The boy butted in, "He means the Nazis!" before whispering, "He thinks the war's still on, remember?"

"Oh, yes, of course," the newsagent whispered back.

"We need some rations, Char Wallah! Quick smart. Need to be back in my Spitfire before dawn."

Raj's eyes darted to the boy for a reaction. Jack shook his head a little, and the newsagent understood that this meant he and the boy needed to have a secret talk.

"Just help yourself, sir!" Raj said to the old man, who proceeded to patter around the shop looking for something to eat. "If you can find any food left, that is. Aunt Dhriti managed to break the door down during the night and scoffed everything in sight. She even took a bite out of the coloring books."

The boy double-checked that his grandfather was out of earshot before speaking.

"I just helped him escape from Twilight Towers."

"Was it as bad as people say?"

"Worse. Much worse. Grandpa thought he was in Colditz Castle, and he wasn't far wrong. But now he wants to take the Spitfire into the skies!"

"You mean the one from the museum?"

"Yes! It's nuts! I just don't know what to say to

him anymore, Raj. Please can you try to talk some sense into him?"

Raj looked lost in thought for a moment.

"Your grandfather was a great war hero. Those were his glory days."

"Yes yes yes, I know," agreed the boy. "But—"

As Grandpa was munching on a half-eaten chocolate bar he'd found on the floor at the far side of the shop, Raj held his finger up. "But but but! Why does there always have to be a but?"

"But—"

"And another one! Jack, your grandfather is a very old man. You know he's getting more and more confused all the time. This thing he has is eating away at his mind."

A tear welled in the boy's eye as the newsagent said this. Raj put his arm around Jack's shoulders.

"It's not fair," declared the boy, as he sniffed back a tear. "Why did it have to happen to my grandpa?"

Raj could be wise if he wanted to. "Jack—the only thing that keeps him going is having you by his side."

"Me?" asked the boy. He didn't understand.

"Yes—you! Whenever he is with you, your grandfather is back in his glory days."

"I suppose so."

"I know so. Listen, I know it's nuts, but it's good to be a little nuts sometimes. Why not let this old hero have his flight?"

Jack wiped away his tears with his sleeve. He looked up at Raj and nodded. In truth, now that the boy had a taste for adventure he longed for more too. Jack had played at being a fighter pilot with his grandfather so many times. Every night he had gone to sleep dreaming of being one.

Now the boy had a chance of making that dream come true.

"Wing Commander!" said the boy.

"Yes, Squadron Leader?" replied Grandpa, completely oblivious to the boy's little chat with Raj.

"Let's take to the skies!"

54

Racing the Sun

Moments later, the three were sat on Raj's beaten-up old motorbike, speeding toward the Imperial War Museum. The faster they went, the more the motorbike rattled. Jack, who was squashed between Raj and his grandfather, was worried the little old thing would shake itself to bits.

They were racing the sun coming up. The hope was that if they could arrive at the museum before dawn, then they had a much better chance of stealing the Spitfire. That way they would still be under the cover of darkness, and with any luck the gorilla-esque security guard would not have started his shift yet.

It was so early all the roads were clear of traffic. In the hour it took to get to the museum, they only passed a few cars, a couple of lorries, and an empty bus. The world had not yet woken up.

Raj dropped the pair off right outside the Imperial War Museum. The place was deserted, save for a flock of pigeons on the roof.

"Good luck up there, Wing Commander, sir," said the newsagent with a salute.

"Thank you, Char Wallah," replied Grandpa with a nod of his head.

"And good luck to you, Squadron Leader." Raj saluted the boy.

"Thank you, Raj…Char Wallah."

"Be safe now, you two! And by the way, there is no charge for that half-eaten chocolate bar you found on the floor of my shop!"

"Most kind," replied Grandpa.

Finally Raj pulled back the throttle hard on his motorbike and rattled off down the road.

So after escaping from one heavily fortified building, Jack and his grandfather now had to break into another. Being full of priceless historical artifacts, the museum had excellent security. A quick sweep around the outside of the building only confirmed what Jack had suspected. All the windows and doors were locked. Last time Grandpa had walked right in because the museum had been open to the public. This time it was not going to be so easy.

By the time the pair came back to the front, they had all but given up hope.

"Some clown has locked up the aircraft hangar!" muttered Grandpa.

Jack looked up at the building. High above the Roman-style columns of the museum front squatted a large green dome. Dotted along the base of it there were a number of small, round windows; they looked like the portholes of a ship. One at the front appeared slightly ajar. Perhaps it could be pried open. But how were they going to get up there?

As Jack pondered this, he leaned on one of the two huge naval cannon that pointed proudly aloft in the courtyard. The boy had an idea.

"Wing Commander?"

"Yes, old boy?"

"If the cannon could be turned around to point the other way, then we could climb along them to reach that open window up there."

The cannon sat on a large metal base. Together the pair tried to push on it, but it just wouldn't turn.

But feeling underneath, Jack found a number of large screws. "I still have the serving spoon, sir!" proclaimed the boy. It was the one he had swiped from the school cafeteria that he hadn't gotten the chance to give to Grandpa earlier that night.

"We can use it as a screwdriver!" said Grandpa.

Using the handle of the spoon, the old man loosened the screws in no time.

With all their strength, the pair then put their shoulders against the base and pushed as hard as they could.

It was tough work, but at last the cannon were pointing up at the museum.

Jack climbed up on to one, while his grandfather heaved himself on to the other. Both held out their arms for balance as they edged their way along. After a few steps, Jack realized it was best not to look down; it was quite a drop.

Eventually Jack and his grandfather reached the roof of the museum. On seeing the Union Jack flying there, Grandpa saluted it, and the boy felt compelled to follow suit.

Pigeon poop covered the roof and it was very slippery, especially if you happened to be wearing slippers.

"This one, sir!" said the boy, indicating the little round window that had been left open ever so slightly. Jack just managed to force his small fingers into the gap, and pulled the window fully open.

"Good work, Squadron Leader!" said Grandpa.

The old man gave the boy a leg up. Jack then reached down his hand to help his grandfather inside.

The pair had broken into the Imperial War Museum.

The feeling landed on Jack like an enormous YES!

Now all they had to do was steal the Spitfire.

55

Driving a Tank

Jack and his grandfather raced down the staircase and into the Great Room of the museum where the aircraft were suspended from the ceiling.

The fighter planes had been repaired since the pair's last visit. The Spitfire had been restored to her former glory.

On the wall was a winch, and the two worked double quick to bring the warbird back down to earth.

In a nearby glass cabinet stood a display of RAF pilots' flying gear on mannequins. Thinking fast, they pushed an old World War I cavalry cannon, that in its day would have been drawn by a horse, toward the cabinet. The cannon smashed the glass.

As if they had been scrambled, the pair raced to put on the flying gear.

The boy checked his reflection in the next glass case along.

GOGGLES—CHECK

HELMET—CHECK

FLYING SUIT—CHECK

SCARF—CHECK

BROWN LEATHER JACKET—CHECK

BOOTS—CHECK

GLOVES—CHECK

PARACHUTE—CHECK

They had their flying suits on.

The Spitfire was on the ground.

But amid all the excitement, the pair had forgotten something.

Something big.

"Wing Commander?" said the boy.

"Yes, Squadron Leader?"

"How are we going to get the plane out of here?"

The old man glanced all around, a look of puzzlement on his face. "Whichever clown designed this aircraft hangar forgot to put the doors in!"

Suddenly it was as if a balloon had been deflated inside Jack. Getting into the museum had been hard enough, but getting the Spitfire out seemed impossible.

On the other side of the hall, a World War I tank was on display. It was a British Mark V, military green with two huge caterpillar tracks. It was so big and heavy, it looked like it could smash through concrete.

Suddenly Jack had an idea. "Do you know how to drive a tank, sir?" asked the boy.

"No! But how hard can it be?" Grandpa was a man who could take everything in his stride.

The pair hurried over to the tank, clambered up, and opened the hatch at the top. Plunging down into the cramped cockpit, they were greeted by the most unfamiliar array of pedals and levers.

"Let's just try a few of these, shall we?" announced Grandpa.

After starting the engine the old man pulled down on a lever, which immediately threw the tank into reverse.

"Make it stop!" shouted Jack.

It was too late. The Imperial War Museum's gift shop had been destroyed.

CRASH!!

Now in something of a panic, the boy pulled the nearest handle and the ancient tank surged forward at terrific speed.

SMASH!!

It demolished the wall of the museum with laughable ease.

Getting the hang of the Mark V now, the pair drove the tank backward and forward a few times to make sure the hole was big enough for the Spitfire's wings to fit through.

SMASH!! Bang! CRASH!

Then they scrambled out of the tank and rushed back over to the Spitfire. They leaped up on to the wing and climbed into the cockpit. As with most World War II fighter planes there was just one seat, so the boy sat on his grandfather's lap.

"Cozy in here, isn't it,
Squadron Leader?"
remarked the old man.

For the first time in his life
Jack was sitting in a real
Spitfire. His dream was coming true.

After all those years of playing pilots with his
grandfather, the inside of the plane was exactly as the
old man had described.

There was an instrument panel with dials for speed
and altitude.

Below that was a compass.

The gun sights were of course at head height.

Between the boy's knees was the control column.
At the top of the stick was the most thrilling part—
a button to fire the machine guns.

Grandpa went through his checks.

"Canopy secure? Check!

"Propeller set to low? Check!

"Battery on? Check!

"Flaps up and trimmed?

"Navigation equipment?

"Flight instruments? Check!

"Fuel? Fuel? **Empty!**"

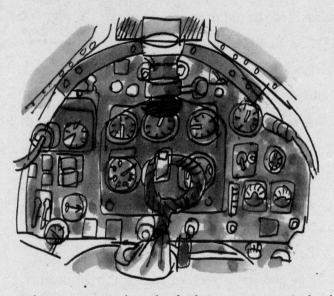

Jack's eyes turned to the fuel gauge. It was indeed empty. Here they were, all dressed up with nowhere to go.

"You stay here, Squadron Leader," said Grandpa.

"What are you going to do?" asked the boy.

"One of us is going to have to get out and push!"

56

Fill Her Up!

The boy sat in the pilot's seat steering, as Grandpa used all his might to push the fighter plane out of the museum and along the road. Luckily most of it was downhill.

The pair were in search of a petrol station, as they needed to fill the plane up with fuel if they were going to take to the air.

Fortunately they soon found one, a little way down the road from the museum.

The lady behind the counter stared, mouth open with shock, as the World War II fighter plane was wheeled on to the forecourt.

From the cockpit Jack shouted down, "Are you sure normal car petrol will be all right for the Spitfire, Wing Commander?"

"She's not going to like it, Squadron Leader!" said Grandpa. "The old girl's going to cough and splutter

a bit. But she will still go."

Needless to say, an airplane needs a great deal more fuel than a car.

The boy watched anxiously as the price on the pump went past one hundred pounds to two hundred, then three, then four.

"Have you got any money with you, sir?" inquired Jack.

"No. Have you?"

Eventually the old man could feel that the fuel tank was full, just as the price reached £999. So he thought he might as well round it up to £1,000. But Grandpa pushed too hard on the pump and the price clicked up to £1,000.01.

"Darn it!" shouted the old man.

"How are we going to pay?"

"I'll just tell the lady that we are on official RAF business. As there is a war on, we have commandeered the fuel."

"Good luck with that, sir!"

The old man didn't understand the sarcasm and marched over to the payment hatch.

At that moment, a little yellow car pulled up at the next pump. From the cockpit, Jack saw that sat in the driving seat was the huge, hairy security guard from the Imperial War Museum. The man was in his uniform, presumably on his way to work.

"Grandpa! I mean, Wing Commander!" the boy shouted.

"Excuse me, madam," said the old man, before turning to his grandson, eyebrows raised. "What is it now, Squadron Leader?"

"I think you better get back in the plane! Quick!"

The security guard had climbed out of his car, ready to confront the boy.

"Oi! You!"

"Just had word on the radio, sir!" cried the boy in desperation. "We must take off at once!"

Grandpa started running toward the plane, shouting instructions. "Righty ho, then! Start her up!"

From all those simulations in his grandfather's flat, Jack knew exactly where the right button was. He pressed it, and the forty-year-old warbird shuddered back into life.

"What on earth do you two think you are doing now?" shouted the security guard over the roar of the engine.

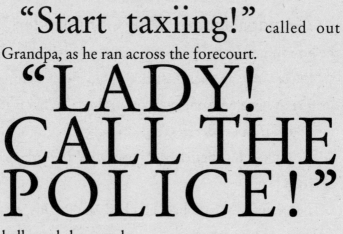

"Start taxiing!" called out Grandpa, as he ran across the forecourt.

"LADY! CALL THE POLICE!" bellowed the guard.

As the Spitfire started taxiing out of the garage, Grandpa ran after it and leaped on to the wing.

The rather hefty security guard initially gave chase on foot, but soon got a stitch and limped back to his car to give chase.

The Spitfire was now taxiing at some speed down the road, as Grandpa shuffled his way along the wing to the cockpit.

Jack had just completed his Highway Code badge on his trike, and when he saw a traffic light turn red ahead, he slammed on the brakes.

The little yellow car pulled up beside them, and the security guard started shouting angrily at the pair.

Jack wasn't sure what to do, so he just smiled and waved.

"What are you stopping for, old boy?" shouted Grandpa. "GO

GO

GO!"

The old man managed to clamber into the cockpit. As he slid the canopy over their heads, he strapped in, took the controls and the fighter plane roared off.

The Spitfire made her way along the main road on the south side of the River Thames.

There were cars hurtling down the road toward them. As if this was a deadly game of dare, Grandpa managed to swerve the plane out of the way of the oncoming vehicles just in time, over and over.

Above the din of the engine, Jack could hear sirens. A way off at first, but getting nearer and nearer.

Nee naw
Nee naw.

The boy looked over his shoulder to see that there was a fleet of police cars in hot pursuit.

"She needs a long stretch of open road to take off!" said Grandpa. But this being Central London, there wasn't one.

Jack looked to his right. More roads. Then he looked to his left and saw Waterloo Bridge come into view.

"Take a left, Wing Commander!"

"Roger!"

The plane spun left and was soon powering its way across the bridge, as if it was a runway.

As they sped along, Jack saw a number of police cars approaching from the far end of the bridge, trying to head them off.

"Look, sir!"

Grandpa increased his speed as the police cars started creating a makeshift roadblock. If the Spitfire didn't take to the air any second now, it was going to SMASH SLAP BANG into them...

57

ZOOM!

WHOOSH!

A huge sense of relief washed over the boy as he realized that he and his grandfather were now airborne.

"Up, *up, and away!*" said the old man.

"Up, *up, and away!*" repeated Jack.

The back wheels on the Spitfire's undercarriage just clipped the roof of one of the police cars in the roadblock, causing the plane to wobble a little. But they were clear.

Now they were heading straight toward the historic Savoy Hotel. But Grandpa pulled the control column back and the plane shot up high in the sky. The old man couldn't help but show off to

the policemen on the ground and performed a victory
roll in the plane.

This was much like a killer whale leaping above the waves just to prove its absolute superiority over every other living thing.

The Spitfire was like that. She was the greatest warplane ever built. And behind the controls was one of the RAF's greatest ever pilots.

In Grandpa's hands, the old plane handled like a brand-new racing car. She could turn on a sixpence; Grandpa flew so close to St Paul's Cathedral his grandson's heart nearly missed a beat. Then the fighter plane powered along the River Thames past HMS *Belfast*, straight toward Tower Bridge. Just as the two sides of the bridge were opening, Grandpa accelerated the Spitfire, and she zoomed straight through.

WHOOSH!

For the first time in his short life, Jack felt truly alive. Free.

"She is all yours, Squadron Leader," said Grandpa.

The boy couldn't believe his ears. His grandfather was giving him control of the fighter plane.

"If you are sure, Wing Commander?"

"Roger!"

With that, the old man took his hands away from the control column and the boy held it tight. Just as his grandfather had taught him, he only needed to make the tiniest of movements for the plane to respond.

Jack wanted to touch the sky. He pulled the control column back and the plane raced up, up, and up. They sped through some clouds and there was the sun. A ball of blazing fire lighting up the sky.

Above the clouds they were alone at last. London was far below them, above them only space.

"I want to do a loop-the-loop, sir!"

"Roger!"

Then the boy pulled the lever sharply toward him and the plane arced in the sky. Now they were upside down! Nothing else mattered aside from this

moment. All of the past and all of the future meant nothing next to this.

Keeping his hands on the control column, the plane was soon the right way up again. Had that been seconds? Minutes?

Nothing mattered. Nothing else mattered. Nothing that had ever happened before mattered. Nothing that was ever going to happen mattered. All there was, was NOW.

The boy took in every single thing. The force pinning him to the seat. The sound of the engine. The smell of the petrol.

The Spitfire leveled out and skimmed the clouds, heading straight for the sun.

Then out of the blinding red light ahead of them, they could see two mysterious black dots emerging. The light was so blinding, it was impossible at first to see what these dots were. But they were traveling at speed toward them.

58

Never Surrender

As the dots drew closer, the boy recognized two Harrier Jump Jets. These were modern jet-powered fighter planes, and they whooshed past the Spitfire at incredible speed.

Jack was scared—what had these fighter planes been sent up to do? Shoot them down? The pair of Harriers flew so close it felt like a warning of some sort. Behind him, he could see the two planes turning back around. In seconds they caught up with them, and flew alongside the Spitfire. One plane on either side, so close that the Harriers' wings were very nearly touching theirs. The Jump Jet pilots wore black visors on their helmets so you couldn't see their eyes, and their mouths were covered by masks. They looked more like robots than people.

"Jerry's got a brand-spanking-new plane!" said Grandpa.

Jack looked to his left, then right.

The pilots on either side were gesturing for them to descend.

"Sir, they are telling us to land," shouted the boy.

"What did Churchill say, Squadron Leader?"

Jack knew from his history lessons that the World War II Prime Minister, Winston Churchill, had said a great many memorable things. Right now he wasn't sure which one in particular his grandfather meant.

"'Never in the field of human conflict was so much owed by so many to so few'?"

"No."

"'We shall fight on the beaches'?"

"No."

Jack was racking his brain. "'I have nothing to offer but blood, toil, tears, and sweat'?"

"No. Not that one," replied Grandpa, getting increasingly confused. "Our great Prime Minister said something about not giving up. I can't recall exactly what he said but I am darn well sure he said we were never to do it!"

"'We shall never surrender'?" ventured the boy.

"That's the one! And I never will..."

The boy gulped in fear.

59

Pure Poetry

The old man pulled back on the control lever and the Spitfire shot up like a rocket. The two Harrier Jump Jet pilots were caught off guard for a moment, before giving chase. The Spitfire's wooden propeller should have been no match for a modern jet engine. But in Grandpa's hands this ancient plane could outmaneuver the Harrier. Yes, the old girl rattled, and  she coughed and spluttered at times. Yet in flight, the Spitfire was pure poetry.

All of a sudden, one of the chasing Harrier Jump Jets launched a missile that whizzed past the Spitfire and exploded in the sky.

BOOM!

It was clearly meant only as a warning.

If they wanted to, the Harriers could shoot the Spitfire down in the blink of an eye. Still, a sense of dread crashed down over Jack.

An unidentified fighter plane flying over Central London was a major security risk. The Jump Jets really had been sent up to bring them down.

At that moment, a voice came over the Spitfire's radio.

"This is Harrier Red Leader. Spitfire, you are flying in restricted airspace. You must land immediately. Over!"

"We will never surrender! Over!" replied Grandpa.

"We do not wish to harm you, but we have orders to shoot you down if you don't! Over!"

"Over and out!" said the old man before turning off the radio.

60

Speeding Through Fire

Behind them Jack and his grandpa could hear another missile being launched. The old man turned the plane on its side and the rocket skimmed past the Spitfire's belly.

BOOM!

The second missile exploded right in front of the Spitfire's nose. Jack closed his eyes as the plane sped through the fire.

"You must do what they say!"

shouted the boy over the deafening noise of the explosion.

"I'd rather die up here a hero than yield and live like a slave on the ground."

"BUT—!"

"You must bail out, though, Squadron Leader!"

shouted Grandpa over the noise.

"I am not leaving you, Grandpa!"

"Grandpa?" Suddenly the old man sounded confused.

"Yes. Grandpa," repeated the boy. "It's me, Jack— your grandson."

"You are my…
grandson?"

"That's right."

"Jack?" asked
the old man.

For a moment it seemed Grandpa was totally present in the here and now.

"Yes. Jack."

"My wonderful grandson. Jack! I can't let you get hurt. You must bail out now."

"I don't want to leave you!" cried the boy.

"But I must leave you."

"Please, Grandpa, I don't want you to die!"

"I love you, Jack."

"I love you, Grandpa."

"As long as you love me, I can never die."

With that, the old man turned the plane upside down, pulled back the canopy and yanked on the boy's parachute cord.

"Up, up, and away!"

shouted Grandpa after his grandson, giving him one last salute.

61

Down to Earth

At once, the parachute opened, and the drag plucked Jack from the fighter plane. The two Harrier Jump Jets thundered past him as he watched the Spitfire climb higher and higher.

As the boy descended back to earth, he stared up at the sky. Soon the Spitfire became nothing more than the tiniest dot in the distance. Soon that dot disappeared from sight altogether.

"Up, *up, and away,*" said the boy to himself, tears streaming down his face.

When Jack looked down he saw London coming into view. The busy metropolis was peaceful from up here. The river, the parks, the roofs of all the great buildings were neatly packed next to each other like squares on a board game.

One sunny afternoon in Grandpa's flat they had played at parachuting out of a stricken Spitfire. So despite never having done it before, the boy knew exactly how to steer himself down to safety by pulling on the parachute's lines.

Jack spied a wide-open space below him. There was lots of greenery, so he assumed it was a park. He guided himself down in its direction to be assured of a soft landing.

DOWN

DOWN

DOWN
the boy sailed.

Soon Jack passed the tops of tall trees. Remembering to bend his knees, he hit the ground at last, and rolled on the neatly cut grass. He lay there, utterly exhausted. For a moment he closed his eyes. It had been a long night.

Without warning, he felt something wet and warm on his face. The boy opened his eyes to see a number of small dogs, all licking him back to life. After a moment, he realized all the dogs were in fact corgis. Jack sat up with a start. From a distance, he saw a rather posh-looking lady neatly dressed in a tweed skirt, quilted jacket, and headscarf. When she moved closer, Jack realized where he had seen her face before.

On a stamp.

It was the Queen.

Behind her was the unmistakeable outline of her magnificent home.

The boy had landed in the garden of Buckingham Palace.

The Queen peered down at Jack and mused, "Aren't you a little young to be in my Royal Air Force?"

PART IV

THE WAY TO THE STARS

62

Salute to a Hero

Grandpa's funeral was a week later. The local church was packed out with those wanting to pay their final respects to this hero.

Jack was sitting in the front row in a pew, between his mother and father. The boy knew the coffin he was staring at was empty. Mysteriously, the Spitfire had never been found. Neither had Grandpa's body.

The Harrier Jump Jet pilots reported seeing the old plane flying higher and higher into the earth's atmosphere, before disappearing from their radar screens. There were days and nights of searches, but all without a trace of the Spitfire turning up anywhere.

A Union Jack was draped over the coffin. It was the British way to honor those in the military. Sat on the coffin was Grandpa's most illustrious medal, the Distinguished Flying Cross.

Directly behind Jack sat Raj, who was crying and blowing his nose loudly like he was playing the tuba. Along from him sat all the elderly people that Grandpa and Jack had rescued from Twilight Towers, including Mrs. Trifle, the Major, and the Rear Admiral. All were forever grateful to the man who had helped them escape—Grandpa.

What happened at Twilight Towers had become something of a national scandal. It had made the front page of the newspapers and the television news. Jack didn't want to take any of the credit, but Grandpa had become **famous**.

The old folk's home may have burned to the ground, but the "nurses" were still at large. What's more, no one knew what fate had befallen the mastermind of it all, Twilight Towers's wicked matron. Had Miss Swine perished in the fire? Or was she busy hatching her next *evil plan?*

On the other side of the aisle, a squadron of old World War II pilots were seated. These elderly comrades of Wing Commander Bunting sat proudly with their backs perfectly straight. All of them had some kind of military mustache, be it the…

Pencil

Handlebar

Muttonchop

Horseshoe

Imperial

Dandy

Swashbuckler

Walrus

Mexican

Lampshade

Toothbrush

French-style

Bat-wing

Fu Manchu

or the Salvador
Dalí.

All wore blazers and slacks, with rows upon rows of medals clinking together on their chests.

All the children from Jack's history class were there too. They had petitioned their teacher, Miss Verity, to have time off their lessons to pay their respects. They had loved Grandpa's visit and would never forget his thrilling stories of the Battle of Britain. Of course, the children wanted to support their classmate Jack too.

On learning what a true hero the old man was, Miss Verity felt mightily guilty at how she had treated him in history class that day. Now she was shedding a tear for him as well. Putting a comforting arm around her was the security guard from the Imperial War Museum. Romance had clearly blossomed between the pair since she gave him the kiss of life.

Behind them on the back pew were Beef and Bone, the two hapless detectives from Scotland Yard. They had gotten to know Jack and his parents well now that they were heading up the police investigation into Twilight Towers. Having seen their interrogation technique, Jack did not hold out much hope. However, the boy knew they meant well and even in his deep sadness he was pleased they could attend Grandpa's funeral too.

After some music from the church organ, Reverend Hogg began his sermon.

"Dearly beloved, we are gathered here today to mourn the passing of a grandfather, a father, and a friend to many."

"He was the only man I ever truly loved!" announced Mrs. Trifle suddenly with a huge sense of melodrama.

But as the boy stared at the vicar, he stopped listening to what he was saying. Jack had begun to notice that there was something very **suspicious** about the man.

63

Broken Noses

As the boy stared, he spotted that the vicar was wearing thick patches of makeup on his face, as if to cover something up. What's more, Reverend Hogg kept stealing nervous glances at Jack from behind his glasses as he spoke. His diamond-encrusted gold watch jangled on his wrist, and when he saw the boy staring at it he pulled his sleeve down awkwardly to hide it. Reverend Hogg's shiny black shoes looked like they were made from hugely expensive alligator skin. Oozing from him was the sickly sweet aroma of champagne and expensive cigars. This was no ordinary vicar who helped others. This was someone who helped himself.

"Now turn to page 124 in your hymn books, 'I Vow to Thee, My Country'."

Reverend Hogg nodded at the organist, a big burly

man with "LOVE" and "HATE" tattooed
on his knuckles. In a sudden flash Jack
realized he was a dead ringer for…
Nurse Rose!

As the music began, all the
mourners rose to their feet and began
to sing.

"I vow to thee, my country, all earthly things above,
"Entire and whole and perfect, the service of my
love…"

During the hymn, Jack gazed at
the vicar's eyes. They were small
and piggy. He had seen those eyes
somewhere else.

"I heard my country calling, away across the sea,
"Across the waste of waters she calls and calls to me."

As the hymn continued, the boy took in the choir.
Scars down their faces, broken noses, teeth missing.

Not one of them knew a single word of the hymn and they mumbled their way through it in low growly voices. Could the one in the middle with the gold tooth be…Nurse Daisy?

"I hear the noise of battle, the thunder of her guns,
"I haste to thee my mother, a son among thy sons."

Jack looked over his shoulder to see the vicar's helper, the verger, standing at the back. As was traditional, he wore a long black gown, but more unusually he had a shaved head and a tattoo of a spider's web across his neck. Again, he looked very familiar. Was this Nurse Blossom?

"And there's another country, I've heard of long ago,

"*Most dear to them that love her, most great to them that know…*"

As the hymn drew to an end, Jack was sure he was close to solving the mystery. Memories flashed through his mind…Miss Swine smoking that big fat cigar, the vicar's zeal in recommending Twilight Towers, that little upturned nose they shared… And if all these church helpers, the organist, the choir, and the verger, were Twilight Towers's fake nurses—the criminal gang, intent on stealing the life savings of the elderly people that they were meant to be looking after—then surely their leader wouldn't be far away.

Continuing with the service, Reverend Hogg announced, "I am now going to read Psalm 33, 'Sing joyfully to the Lord'…"

Jack couldn't contain himself any longer and rose to his feet.

"STOP THE FUNERAL!"

he bellowed.

64

Pants on Fire!

Stopping a funeral midway through was unheard of. None of the people gathered in the church could believe the boy had done it. Suddenly all eyes in the room were on Jack. Except one or two wandering glass eyes that belonged to the elderly airmen.

"What is the meaning of this?" thundered Reverend Hogg.

"What on earth are you doing, son?" whispered Dad.

"Please, Jack, just sit down and be quiet!" hissed Mum, pulling the boy by the arm to sit back down on the pew.

"The vicar…" began the boy. He was trembling slightly and as much as he tried to, he couldn't quite keep his finger from wobbling.

"The vicar and the matron…they…they are…THE SAME PERSON!"

GASP!

Four hundred people gasped in shock. Except the Rear Admiral who was more than a little deaf, and as his hearing aid whistled loudly he called out, "What did you say, boy?"

"I said," began Jack again, much louder this time, "THE VICAR AND THE MATRON ARE THE SAME PERSON. HE'S A CROOK!"

"Sorry. Someone was whistling in my ear. I didn't hear a ruddy word."

His friend the Major was sat right next to him and shouted, **"HE SAID THE VICAR IS A CROOK!"**

"A COOK?" The Rear Admiral was not getting it at all. **"WHAT DOES HE COOK?"**

"I'LL EXPLAIN LATER!"

bellowed the Major.

"No, I, er, that vile little child is lying!" protested the vicar now. Sweat beaded on his forehead. His mouth was so dry it had started making clicking sounds when he tried to speak. The man was unraveling like a ball of string.

Meanwhile the choir looked at each other nervously. They had been rumbled.

"HE MADE US DO IT!" cried "Nurse Daisy" suddenly. "PRETEND TO BE NURSES AT AN OLD FOLK'S HOME!"

"SILENCE!" snapped the vicar.

"I'LL CONFESS EVERYTHING! I AM TOO PRETTY FOR PRISON!"

"I SAID SILENCE!"

One of the rats was already leaving the sinking ship. More were sure to follow. The boy felt he was on a roll now. "So 'Miss Swine' did survive the fire at Twilight Towers after all! You have been hiding in plain sight all this time!"

"I have done nothing wrong!" protested Reverend Hogg. "I only changed their wills so I could give all the money to the poor!"

"Liar! Liar!" shouted the boy.

"Pants on fire!" continued Raj.

"You spent what you stole on champagne and cigars and a brand-new sports car!" exclaimed Jack.

Reverend Hogg had been well and truly **BUSTED**.

65

An Army of Oldies

As he stood at the altar, the vicar's tone became angry and bitter. "So what if I did, child? What use was all their money anyway to the stupid old farts?"

Needless to say, this did not go down well in a room full of elderly people. The church was soon bristling with angry murmurs.

"After every Sunday service I would empty the collection tin. All the miserable old fools would give me was a few copper coins and an old button. How could I buy a holiday home in Monte Carlo on that?"

"OH, BOO HOO HOO!"

heckled Raj sarcastically.

"Shut your face, you!" shouted the vicar.

" Ooooooooh!" mocked Raj.

"So I hatched a plan with my gravediggers. I would start my own old folk's home, and forge new wills for all the old stinkers, making their money MINE…"

"Could you talk a bit slower, please?" called out Detective Beef from the back, a notebook in his hand. "I am trying to write all this down." Detective Bone rolled his eyes.

"You are a wicked, wicked man!" shouted Jack.

"And woman!" added Mrs. Trifle.

"Yes! And woman!" cried the boy. "A wicked, wicked man and a wicked, wicked woman. You treated all the old folk with incredible cruelty!"

"Oh, who cares about them?! They were all completely gaga!"

Needless to say, this did not go down well in the room either.

"HOW DARE YOU!" exclaimed Mrs. Trifle.

"GET HIM!" ordered the Major.

"CHARGE!" shouted the Rear Admiral.

With that, the old folk in the church rose to their feet and began stampeding toward the vicar and his gang.

"Let the police handle this!" shouted Detective Bone. But the ex-residents of *Twilight Towers* were in no mood to listen. They wanted REVENGE. As the crooks tried to flee the church, the old folk chased after them. Walking sticks, handbags, Zimmer frames…all became weapons. Mrs. Trifle began whacking the vicar as hard as she could with a hymn book. Meanwhile, the Major had cornered the verger

(aka "Nurse Blossom") and pinned him against the wall with the lectern. The Rear Admiral had both "nurses" Rose and Daisy in headlocks, as Wing Commander Bunting's old RAF colleagues lined up to whack them over their heads with prayer cushions.

The children from Jack's history class all cheered.

This criminal gang didn't stand a chance against an army of oldies.

"I must come to church more often," commented Raj. "I never knew it could be so much fun!"

66

Good-bye

Jack's parents looked on at all the chaos unfolding in the church, and then turned to their son.

"I am sorry we didn't believe you at first, Jack," said Mum.

"You are a very brave boy to take on an evil crook like that, son," added Dad. "I know Grandpa would have been very proud of you."

On hearing that, Jack wanted to smile and cry at the same time. So he did both.

Seeing her son's tears, Mum put her arms around the boy. Despite the strong pong of Stinking Bishop (an eye-wateringly smelly cheese), it felt good.

Dad put his arms around both of them, and for a moment everything seemed right in the world.

The running battle between the gang of heavies and the army of oldies was now spilling outside into the churchyard. Jack's classmates excitedly followed the action as the two detectives tried and failed to restore law and order.

"I should go home and start making the cheese sandwiches," said Mum. "Everyone is meant to be coming back to ours after the service."

"Yes," agreed Dad, "and these old folk are working up quite an appetite. Come on, son."

"Go on ahead," replied the boy. "I just want to stay here a moment longer on my own."

"Oh yes, I understand," said Mum.

"Right you are, son," said Dad. He took his wife's hand and together they made their way out of the church.

Now it was completely empty of people, save for Jack and Raj. The newsagent put his hand on the boy's shoulder.

"What an adventure you have had, young Master Bumting."

"I know, but I couldn't have done it without Grandpa."

The newsagent smiled, before saying, "And he couldn't have done it without you. I'll leave you alone with him now. I imagine you want to say your final farewell."

"Thank you. I do."

True to his word, Raj left the boy alone in the church with his grandfather's empty coffin.

Jack looked at the wooden box and flag, and saluted one last time.

"Good-bye, Wing Comm—" he began, before correcting himself. "I mean, good-bye, Grandpa."

Epilogue

That night Jack lay in bed, in the place just between awake and asleep. The room was beginning to disappear to make way for the world of dreams.

Then outside his window the boy heard a far-off sound. The hum of an aircraft high in the sky. Jack opened his eyes, and slid down from the top bunk. So as not to wake his parents asleep in the next room,  he tiptoed over to the window and silently pulled back the curtains. Framed by a silvery moon was the unmistakeable silhouette of a Spitfire. She swooped and twirled. She rolled. She danced in the air. There could only be one man behind the controls.

"Grandpa?!" exclaimed Jack.

The airplane began a thrilling descent and zoomed past the boy's window. There in the cockpit sat Wing Commander Bunting. As the gleaming fighter plane rocketed past, Jack noticed the strangest thing of all. His grandfather looked exactly as he did in the photograph above the boy's bed. The one taken in 1940, when Grandpa was a young pilot, fighting in the Battle of Britain. He was young again. The WHOOSH of the Spitfire made Jack's model airplanes wobble. He looked on as the Spitfire climbed high into the night sky. Eventually, she disappeared out of sight.

The boy told no one. Who would believe him anyway?

The next night as Jack climbed into bed, he was breathless with excitement. Would he see his grandfather again? He closed his eyes and concentrated as hard as he could. Once again, in that place just between awake and asleep, the boy heard the roar of the Spitfire's engine. Once again she sped past his window.

And the next night. And the next. Every night it was the same story.

It was just as the old man had said. As long as Jack loved him, Grandpa could never die.

*

Today Jack is all grown up and has a young son too. As soon as the boy was old enough, Jack told him all about his amazing adventures with his grandfather. At bedtime the boy would ask again and again for the stories of the daring escape from Twilight Towers, or the theft of the fighter plane, or the parachute drop into the garden of Buckingham Palace. And now when the boy drifts off to sleep, he too can see the Spitfire in the sky. Every night she zooms past his window before shooting off toward the stars.

Up, up, and away.

The End

Glossary

The 1940s

The 1940s were dominated by World War II and its aftermath. It was a decade of great change and upheaval for the British public as millions of soldiers joined the Armed Forces to fight, while those who stayed at home had to adjust to new rules and ways of life to help the war effort. Everyone was called upon to "do their bit" to help the nation and people were encouraged to "make do and mend," which meant reusing and repairing clothes and furniture instead of throwing them away. After the war ended, in 1945, life didn't return to normal right away. Clothes rationing lasted until 1949 and the UK was nearly bankrupted by debts that had accumulated during the war, so living conditions were poor.

World War II

World War II began in 1939 and ended in 1945. The war was fought between the Axis powers (including

Germany, Italy and Japan) and the Allies (including Britain, France, the USA, Canada, India, China, and the Soviet Union). Interestingly the Soviet Union—largely made up of Russia—began the war on the Axis side. War was declared in 1939 when German forces illegally invaded Poland, which Britain and France had promised to protect. The war brought dramatic changes to ordinary people's lives in Britain, where over two million children were evacuated from the cities to the countryside so that they would be safe from German air raids, in which many homes were destroyed. Food and other goods were greatly limited as people left their jobs to join the war effort. The countries that were invaded by the Axis powers suffered even greater devastation.

On June 6, 1944, known as D-Day, Allied forces landed in Normandy to free France from German control. After that, the soldiers fought their way into Germany and the war in Europe came to an end in May 1945. The Allies continued to fight the Japanese in the Pacific until August. An Allied victory was officially declared on September 2, 1945, and World War II was over.

Winston Churchill

Winston Churchill is probably the most celebrated political leader in British history. He served as Prime Minister during World War II. After leaving school with poor exam results he became a soldier and part-time journalist before moving into politics. His military leadership was decisive in the eventual Allied victory, and the stirring speeches he gave to the British people, broadcast on the radio, were incredibly important in keeping up the morale of the nation. He died in 1965, aged ninety, and was awarded the huge honor of a state funeral by the Queen.

Adolf Hitler

Adolf Hitler was the head of the National Socialist, or Nazi, Party and seized power as Chancellor of Germany in 1933. Immediately he made changes to give himself total control and remove anyone who might oppose him. Hitler believed in the absolute supremacy of the German people and this belief ultimately led to him ordering the mass murder of millions of Jews, Gypsies, and other minority groups. Known as the Holocaust, this remains one of the darkest events in the history of the human race. Trapped in his bunker as Russian soldiers entered Berlin in 1945, Hitler shot himself.

The Gestapo

Formed in 1933, the Gestapo was the name given to the feared German secret police. Its purpose was to find and arrest enemies of Hitler's government, and its members were given special powers to imprison people at their own will, and make them talk. Because of this they earned a reputation for being utterly ruthless.

Rationing

Food rationing was introduced in Britain in January 1940 as a way of making sure there was enough to go round for everyone during the war. To buy particular foods, ration coupons were used alongside money so that no one could buy more than their share. In 1940, rationed foods included sugar, meat, tea, butter, bacon, and cheese—but many more were rationed later. While fruit and vegetables were never rationed they were often hard to obtain and the government encouraged people to grow them in their gardens. Other rationed goods included petrol, soap, and even clothes.

Colditz Castle

Colditz Castle in Germany was used by the Nazis as a prisoner-of-war camp during World War II. It was thought of as an "inescapable fortress." However, many people did try to escape from Colditz, hatching clever plans involving copied keys, escaping into the sewers, forging identity papers, and even sewing prisoners into mattresses. Most attempts failed, but around thirty escapees were successful.

Operation Sea Lion

After Germany's successful invasion of France in June 1940, Hitler ordered his armed forces to prepare to invade England via ships. This plan was codenamed Operation Sea Lion. To give it the best chance of succeeding, the Germans knew they first had to take control of the skies above England and remove the threat posed by the RAF. This led to the Battle of Britain.

The Battle of Britain and the Blitz

The Battle of Britain began in the summer of 1940. The German Air Force, called the Luftwaffe, launched a series of attacks on England, bombing coastal targets and airfields in an attempt to destroy defenses and leave the country open to invasion. The battle was an epic test of strength between the Luftwaffe and the RAF. While the Germans had more aircraft and pilots, the

British had a very good communication system, which gave the RAF a crucial advantage.

In late August the Luftwaffe wrongly believed that the RAF was near breaking point and turned its attention to bombing London and other British cities. This period was known as the Blitz. For fifty-seven nights in a row German bombs were dropped on British cities, and thousands of people had to seek shelter in Underground stations and air-raid shelters. While this caused terrible damage, it also gave the British time to recover their air defenses.

On September 15 the Luftwaffe suffered major losses at the hands of the RAF. They had failed in their mission and Operation Sea Lion was abandoned soon after. Britain had won its first major victory of the war. The pilots who fought in the Battle of Britain are still celebrated as heroes. If they had lost, it is likely the Nazis would have invaded Britain.

RAF

The Royal Air Force was established in 1918. It played a vital role in helping the Allies win World War II and its most famous campaign was the Battle of Britain.

In 1940 the average age of an RAF pilot was just twenty years old.

Luftwaffe

The Luftwaffe was the name of the German air force. By the summer of 1940 it had become the biggest air force in the world. Going into the Battle of Britain, the German pilots were very experienced and confident that they would defeat the British. The Luftwaffe was disbanded in 1946 after the Germans had lost World War II.

WAAF

WAAF stands for the Women's Auxiliary Air Force— this was formed during World War II as a part of the RAF, but peopled entirely by women. At its peak strength there were over 180,000 members. A member of the WAAF was also called a WAAF. WAAFs did not take part in active combat but they were involved in other crucial roles such as monitoring aircraft radar, crewing the barrage balloons, and working with codes. WAAFs were vital in planning operations, including during the Battle of Britain.

Char Wallah

This was the term used by the British Army stationed in India for the local people who served them tea. In the Hindi language the word "wallah" means someone who performs a certain task; the word "chai" means tea. However, in English this word has often been heard and understood as "char," hence the phrase "Char Wallah."

The Hurricane

The Hurricane was a fighter plane that played a key role in achieving victory over Germany during World War II. They were incredibly strong and had the most endurance—or staying power—of all the fighter planes, although they weren't as quick or maneuverable as the Spitfire. After the war, Hurricanes were retired from military service.

The Messerschmitt

The Messerschmitt was the main plane used by the Luftwaffe during the Battle of Britain. The Messerschmitt was able to dive much faster than the British aircraft. However, it had a much shorter flying time (just thirty minutes) before needing more fuel: a huge disadvantage in battle.

The Spitfire

The Spitfire was designed in the 1930s. The fighter plane was very advanced and could be easily upgraded to deal with new threats. Its adaptability, along with its speed and firepower, made it so successful. The Spitfire was a one-seater monoplane (meaning it had just one set of wings) with a very large nose, or front portion. The RAF used Spitfires for military action right up until 1954. It remains the most legendary British fighter plane ever to take to the skies.

Wishing for more Walliams adventures?

Keep reading for a sneak peek.

CHAPTER 1
MONSTER MAN

"Aaarrrggghhh!" screamed the boy.

The most monstrous face he had ever seen was peering down at him. It was the face of a man, but it was completely lopsided. One side was larger than it should have been, and the other was smaller. The face smiled as if to calm the boy down, only to reveal a set of broken and rotten teeth. This made the boy even more scared than before.

"Aaaaarrrrrggggghhhhh!!!!!" he screamed again.

"You will be all right, young sir. Please try and be calm," slurred the man.

His face was so misshapen, that so was his speech.

Who was this man and where was he taking the boy?

It was only then the boy realized he was lying on his back, staring straight up. It felt almost as if he was floating. But something was **rattling**. *He* was **rattling.** The boy realized he must be lying on a trolley. A trolley with wonky wheels.

His head clouded with questions.

Where was he?

How did he get here?

Why couldn't he remember a thing?

And, most importantly, who was this terrifying man-monster?

The trolley traveled slowly down the long corridor. The boy could hear the sound of something being dragged along the floor. It sounded like the *squeak* of a shoe.

He looked down. The man was limping. Just like his face, one side of his body was smaller than the other,

so the man was dragging his withered leg along with him. It looked like every movement might be painful.

BANG!

A pair of tall doors swung open and the trolley trundled into a room and came to a stop. Then some curtains were drawn around the boy.

"I hope that wasn't too uncomfortable, young sir," said the man. The boy thought it was curious that this man called him "sir." He had never been called "sir" in his life. He was only twelve. "Sir" was a title reserved only for teachers at his boarding school. "Now you wait here. I'm just the porter. Let me get the nurse. Nurse!"

As he lay there, the boy felt strangely disconnected from his own body. It felt limp. Lifeless.

The pain, though, was in his head. It was throbbing. Hot. If the feeling could be a color, it would be red. A bright, hot, raging red.

The pain was so intense he closed his eyes.

When he opened them, he realized he was staring straight up at a bright fluorescent light. This made his head ache even more than before.

Then he heard the sound of footsteps approaching.

The curtain was whisked back.

A large older lady in a blue-and-white uniform with a hat leaned over and examined the boy's head. Dark circles framed her bloodshot eyes. Gray wiry hair squatted on her head. Her face was red raw, as if she had scrubbed it with a cheese grater. In brief, she had the appearance of someone who had not slept for a week, and was angry about it.

"Oh deary me! Oh deary, deary me. Oh deary, deary, deary me…" she muttered to nobody in particular.

In his confused state the boy took a moment to realize this woman was in fact dressed as a nurse.

At last the boy realized where he was. A hospital.

He had never been in one before, except the day he was born. And he couldn't remember that.

The boy's eyes drifted up to the lady's name badge: Nurse Meese, **Lord Funt Hospital**.

"That is a bump. A big bump. A very big bump. Now, does this hurt?" she said as she poked the boy hard on his head with her finger.

"Oooowwww!" he screamed, so loudly it echoed along the corridor.

"Some slight pain," muttered the nurse. "Now, just let me get the doctor. Doctor!"

The curtain was whisked across, and then back again.

As the boy lay there staring at the ceiling, he could

hear the sound of footsteps departing.

"Doctor!" she barked out again, now some way down the corridor.

"Coming, Nurse!" came a voice from far off.

"Quickly!" she shouted.

"Sorry!" said the voice.

Then there was the sound of footsteps approaching at speed.

The curtain was whisked back.

A young pointy-faced man breezed in, his long white coat trailing behind him.

"Oh dear. Oh dear, oh dear," announced a posh voice. It was a doctor, and he was somewhat out of breath at having had to run. Looking up, the boy read the man's name badge – DOCTOR LUPPERS.

"That is a big bump. Does this hurt?" The man took out a pencil from his breast pocket. He then held one end and tapped the boy's head with it.

"Oooowwww!" the boy screamed again. It wasn't as bad as being jabbed by a gnarly old finger, but it still hurt.

"Sorry, sorry, sorry! Please don't report me. I've only just graduated as a doctor, you see."

"I won't," muttered the boy.

"Are you sure?"

"Quite sure!"

"Thank you. Now I need to make sure I cross the 'i's and dot the 't's. I just have this little admissions form to fill in." The man then proceeded to roll out a form that looked as if it might take a week to complete.

The boy sighed.

"So, young man," began the doctor in a singsong tone that he hoped might make this boring task fun, "what is your name?"

The boy's mind went blank.

He had never forgotten his own name before.

"Name?" asked the doctor again.

But, try as he might, the boy couldn't remember it.

"I don't know," he spluttered.

A look of panic swept across the doctor's face. "Oh dear," he said. "There are a hundred and ninety-two questions on this form and we are still stuck on question one."

"I'm sorry," replied the boy. As he lay on the hospital trolley, a tear rolled down his cheek. He felt like such a failure, not even being able to remember his own name.

"Oh no! You're crying!" said the doctor. "Please don't cry! The hospital principal could come by and think that I have upset you!"

The boy did his best to stop. Doctor Luppers searched his pockets for a tissue. Unable to locate one, he dabbed the boy's eyes with the form.

"Oh no! Now the form's wet!" he exclaimed. He

then began blowing on the form to try and dry it. This made the boy laugh. "Oh good!" said the man. "You are smiling! Now, look, I am sure we can find out your name. Does it begin with an **A?**"

The boy was pretty sure it didn't. "I don't think so."

"B?"

The boy shook his head.

"C?"

He shook his head again.

"This could take some time," muttered the doctor under his breath.

"T!" exclaimed the boy.

"You would like a cup of tea?"

"No! My name. It begins with a **T!**"

Doctor Luppers smiled as he wrote the first letter on the top of the form. "Let's see if I can guess. **Tim? Ted? Terry? Tony? Theo? Taj?** No, you don't look like a **Taj**… I've got it! **Tina?!**"

All these suggestions firing at the boy clouded his mind, making it more difficult for him to remember, but finally his own name came shining through.

"Tom!" said Tom.

"Tom!" exclaimed the doctor, as if he was about to have guessed it. He wrote down the next two letters. "So what do they call you? **Thomas? Tommy? Big Tom? Little Tom? Tom Thumb?**"

"Tom," replied Tom wearily. Tom had already said his name was Tom.

"Do you have a surname?"

"It begins with a C," said the boy.

"Well, at least we have the first letter. It's like doing the crossword!"

"Charper!"

"Tom Charper !" said the man, scribbling it down on the form. "That's question one done. Just a hundred and ninety-one to go. Now, who brought you to the hospital today? Are your mummy and daddy here?"

"No," said Tom. He could be sure of that. His parents weren't here. They were never *here*; they were always *there*. For some years now, they had packed their only child off to a posh boarding school deep in the English countryside: ***St. Willet's Boarding School for Boys.***

Tom's father earned a lot of money working in desert countries far away, extracting oil from the ground, and his mother was very good at spending that money. Tom would only see them on school holidays, usually in a different country each time. Even though Tom had traveled alone for hours to see them, his father would often still have to work all day and his mother would leave him with a nanny while she went shopping for more shoes and handbags. The boy would be lavished with presents upon arrival – a new train set, a model plane, or a knight's suit of armor. But with nobody to play with Tom would get bored quickly. All he really wanted was to spend time with Mum and Dad, but time was the one thing they never ever gave him.

Don't miss these books by
David Walliams